DEEP COLD

Eight Stories & One Novella by

Michael Prescott

DEEP COLD

TABLE OF CONTENTS

FOREWORD

This rather ample collection of nine tales is my third compilation of short stories, the first two being *Pitch Black* and *Being Alone Together*. Like the latter, it consists mostly of vignettes, terse stories which merely set scenes or portray a "slice of life" (hence the reason some writers refer to vignettes as "slice-of-life" stories). And as with both previous collections, most of the tales in this volume are quite dark, some of them *extremely* dark, while a few are simply melancholy, centered around broken lives, strained relationships, or deeply troubled characters. One of them, "Italian Lobster," I find both lurid and risible at the same time.

Of all the stories, my favorite is undoubtedly the novella, "The Fortuitous Death of Dr. Alfred W. Preston," with "Room 133" and "Cat in the Moonlight" trailing closely behind. "Fortuitous," with which the volume concludes, is quite different from my usual stories, in that it is almost entirely plot-driven, with numerous twists and turns, and features a large cast of characters varying widely in temperament, dress, diction, social class, and moral complexion.

No story has ever given me greater difficulty, both in terms of its composition and the intricacies of its plot. It also required considerable research into complex matters medical, legal, and historical. It is my hope that the great deal of effort I put into it pays off, particularly in its denouement, with which I struggled fiercely and revised several times. (It turns out that tying plot strands together and concocting clever endings to Poe-esque mysteries, even of a relatively short and straightforward ilk, is not exactly my forte.) So as to avoid spoilers, for those who are interested I have included more detailed notes on the story's origins and arduous construction at the end of the book.

As always, it is my hope that the reader will enjoy these stories as much as I enjoyed writing them, and forgive any morbid indulgences on the part of the author. I hold fast to the principle that the demons we exorcise creatively are far less likely to plague us in our everyday lives, and that true catharsis and literary authenticity sometimes require depictions of brutality from which, if realized, any basically moral human being would shirk in horror. The world can be a profoundly cruel and unforgiving place, in which unthinkable savageries too often occur, and many of the stories gathered here reflect that unfortunate fact. I have always tried to remain true to my characters, true to their emotions and ambitions, whether magnanimous or self-serving, virtuous or violent. The results are not always pretty, I concede, but at least they are honest, refusing to skirt the sometimes appalling extremes of human behavior.

The stories in this tome were written between July 2012 and February 2013, a period in my life during which I overcame myriad hurdles, both emotional and professional. Since I published *Being Alone Together* in June 2012, I am enormously gratified to report that the circumstances of my personal life have dramatically improved. Indeed, but for several fortuitous events (much like those in the tale of Dr. Preston), this book would not even exist.

Finally, as always, thank you to my faithful following of readers for their constancy of support, encouragement, and constructive criticism - and, of course, for their reading my work in the first place. I would like to thank in particular Matthew Brummond and Giuseppe Graziano for their generous contribution of advice and feedback on "Fortuitous." (You'll notice my nod to Mr. Brummond in the scene with the Walbrook innkeeper.) Without their kind assistance, the story would be much different and undoubtedly far worse.

Until we meet again, Dear Reader, enjoy and be well.

Michael J. Prescott
February 15, 2013

ROOM 133

The snow fell briskly, crisp flakes scattering across a dead brown lawn. It was nearly sunrise. The man and the woman stole out of the unpainted frame house with paper bags in their hands. The savage wind bit at their faces, blustered their skin, tousled their hair. They wore old jackets with tears in the sleeves. They had searched for hats but could find none. Elmer knew the sun would be up soon and that Malinda and Randall would wake at first light and hurried to get the bags into the pickup truck. Ladonna watched as she massaged her stomach with red wool mittens, her left pinky poking out of the hole at the tip, perhaps trying to warm the life inside her. The snow grew heavier.

"Get in," Elmer said, squinting against the wind.

"Are we ready?"

"Get in," he said again.

She got in. The stars were fading, the moon almost gone now. Purple light bloomed on the eastern horizon, washing away the night. The snow kept coming in violent sheets, swirling about in the crossing gales, sticking to their boots and jackets and the skin on their faces. Ladonna swept away a melting flake with her tongue.

With the bags parked securely in the back of the truck, Elmer opened the driver's-side door and climbed in. He turned to Ladonna, with pale blue lips and scarlet cheeks, and tried to call up a smile. "You okay?" he asked her.

"Just fine," she said.

"We'll go, then."

"Okay."

He started the truck and they backed down the driveway. As they turned onto the road and Elmer put the truck in drive, a light came on in the living room window. He looked at her again, eyes worried and afraid.

"Just go," she said.

And they went.

They stopped at a filling station three miles outside of town. Elmer put a tank's worth of diesel into the truck. Ladonna sat in the passenger seat, still massaging her stomach. He signaled for her to roll the window down, which she did. He leaned in and asked if she was okay.

"I'm fine," she said, smiling wanly.

"We'll be there in twenty minutes."

"Just hurry up. It's cold."

"Just let me pay for the gas."

She watched him plow his way through a whirlwind of snow and disappear into the store. She heard the bell jingle as the door closed behind him, then rolled up the window. She put her hands back on her stomach, shivering, and waited. Would he always be as good to them as he had been so far? Would he always love them the way he did right now? She could only hope.

He emerged from the store a minute later and slogged through the mantle of snow, his dark face coming slowly into view, his dark eyes half-closed against the onslaught. He was so handsome, so strong. He was everything she'd ever wanted.

"I got some smokes," he said as he climbed into the cab.

"I can't smoke no more," she said.

"I know that, baby."

"But you can."

He just smiled and started the truck's engine. The sudden blast of heat was wonderful, and she closed her eyes, wanting to sleep. It had been a long night.

They arrived at the motel as dawn broke fully. Great mounds of snow had gathered along the roadside, and big drifts had formed in the parking lot. They skidded a little before Elmer finally maneuvered the Chevy into a spot near the door. He cut the engine and looked at her. "We're here," he said.

"Are we doing the right thing, Elmer?"

"I think so, baby."

"You said running away wouldn't solve nothin'."

"I thought about it again."

"And now you think it will?"

"I think it has to," he said.

He got out and went around the truck and opened the door for her and helped her out. The pavement was slick with ice. She wasn't quite showing yet but would be soon. The snow was finally beginning to taper.

"Come on, sweetheart," he said to her.

"I'm coming."

"I hope they have a room."

"They will."

And they did. There were two left, and they took the one nearest the truck. Elmer paid in cash and took the key from the clerk and led Ladonna back outside, down the covered sidewalk to Room 133. He opened the door with the key and let her inside. The room was warm and clean, with a double bed and a color television and a Bible in the drawer. It was all they could have asked for, all they needed right now.

"I'm gonna take a shower," Ladonna said.

"Okay, baby."

She went into the bathroom and Elmer took the Bible from the drawer, started reading Genesis. After a few pages his head hurt and he put the Bible on the end table and listened to the shower run. It stopped a minute or two later. He heard Ladonna cough as she got out.

He had filled her with child two months before, at her parents' house. She'd told him a week afterwards she was pregnant. They were young and had panicked, had devised one plan after another, and rejected them all. Until they'd decided on this one. This one, they knew, would work. This one had to.

She came out with a towel wrapped around her middle and another around her head. "Do you still love me?" she asked him.

"Of course I do."

"Will you always?"

"Of course I will."

She smiled and dried herself and dressed. Elmer turned on the TV. Outside, the sun was up near full. He put on the news, and then a cartoon. He watched it while she did her makeup and got bored and turned it off.

"Honey?" he called to her.

Deep Cold

"Yes, sweetie?"

"Are we doing the right thing?"

She hesitated, lowering her eyeliner pencil for a moment. "You said we were."

"I think we are."

"Then we are."

"All right."

He stood abruptly and donned his jacket and gloves. "I'm gonna go outside and have a smoke," he said.

"Okay, baby."

He slipped outside, quickly closed the door behind him. He lit a cigarette and watched the snow, all but finished now. There were a good six or seven inches on the parking lot. It had been a long and powerful squall. He smoked his cigarette and looked at the hazy sun, still cresting the eastern rim, and rubbed his hands together. The cold was awful, raw and ceaseless, a knife

20

slicing through fine silk. It bit at his face, made his eyes water and stung his cheeks. He brooked it and smoked.

Inside, Ladonna lay down on the bed and looked at the ceiling, enjoying the heat from the vents, wishing Elmer would come back inside so they could make love. This would be their first child, and the thought of raising it made her nervous and scared, but she hoped for many more. She loved Elmer fiercely, loved him desperately, and wanted to spend her life with him. But she still worried. She worried about her parents, and his. She worried about her little brother, about being away from him. And she worried for Elmer, that maybe he wasn't ready yet to be a father.

Elmer dropped his cigarette to the ground and crushed it out with a twist of his boot heel. He opened the door and stepped inside. Ladonna was waiting for him, naked and ready. "Baby," he said.

"Come here."

He went to her, trembling, and took off his gloves. The heat felt good. It felt good to be alone with her, to know her all over again. It felt wonderful to hold her.

There was more snow that night, and as they lay next to each other on the bed, listening to the wind howl, neither of them spoke. They didn't know where they'd go in the morning.

AGORAPHOBIA

Quincy looked out the window, surveying the yard. The wind rippled through the grass, rustling the blades, and through the trees, shaking the leaves. It was autumn, and some of the leaves fell, fluttering to the ground in a shower of red and gold and orange. The house across the street was still, deserted. It was midday, but the sun hid behind a batch of clouds, drawing up the shadows it had cast just minutes before. The neighborhood was quiet today.

Quincy drew the curtains and turned toward the kitchen, hesitated. The kitchen was big, full of cabinets and drawers. There was stove in there, and a fridge, and a microwave, all sorts of things that could hurt him. Better, he thought, to go into the living room, which was smaller and contained only a couch and an arm-chair. He would sit on the couch, he thought, and try not to think about what he had seen, all that vast stillness outside. He would sit on the couch and try his best not to tremble.

So he went into the living room and sat down, slowly, on the couch. He regarded a painting of a clay house with a thatched roof and a path leading from the front door into the woods. He wondered what lurked in those woods, what awful dangers. He imagined living inside that house, and hunkering down in a corner, endeavoring not to be seen. And if some terrific storm came along, some torrential downpour, and melted his abode? If some unthinkable horror emerged from the forest and tore apart his roof? He would rightly squeal, he would, shriek like a little girl who had spotted a mouse.

The living room wasn't safe, he decided, was perhaps even more perilous than the kitchen. He retreated, therefore, into his bedroom, where he sat upon the bed with his face in his hands. Why did such fear consume him? What, exactly, was its source? He couldn't answer such questions, found them baffling and vexatious, batted them away with a mental swat. He had entertained them enough already. He had tried to no avail to answer them. What good did it accomplish to pose them over and over again, to torture himself with them?

The bed was comfortable, safe. He took a pen and a piece of paper and laid the latter upon the cover of a book, began to scribble his name over and over again. Then he wrote: "I am safe in here; nothing can get me; there is nothing to fear." He wrote this twenty-six times, but knew it was a lie. He was *not* safe in his room; *anything* could get him; and there was *everything* to fear.

A nasty sweat broke out on his brow. His heart began to pound. His breath caught in his throat. He needed to get out of there, get to someplace smaller and more protective. But moving seemed impossible.

Just go, he thought.

I can't. I'll throw up.

Go now before it's too late.

Retching, he stood and raced into the bathroom, as if a swarm of bees were after him. He slammed the door against thin air, locked it, and leaned back against the wall.

Safety, at last.

He took a long, deep breath, his legs shaking violently. He closed his eyes and pictured the leaves outside, blowing across the lawn, varying in size and color and shape, tumbling about at mother nature's whim. He pictured the lawn itself, browning grass starved of sunlight, blades once lush green now withering quietly, compliantly under the harsh press of an approaching winter. He pictured his neighbor's house: it was empty because its resident had left it, had ventured outside. When had he last done the same?

You stay inside because it's safe.

You're losing your mind.

Both voices were right; both spoke the truth. The result was monstrous confusion and disquietude on Quincy's part. The result was virtual paralysis.

You're not safe in here, either.

But surely he was. Surely he must be. It was, after all, his bathroom, the smallest room in the house. If he wasn't safe in *here*, then where *would* he be?

Get in the bathtub.

He looked at it, the porcelain reservoir in which he'd last showered a week ago. The curtain was pulled back halfway. Fresh beads of sweat rose on his forehead and spilled down his cheeks. His legs were still quivering. His eyes were strained, bulging in their sockets. His hair poked up in quills and jags.

Get in the bathtub. It's the only place you'll be safe.

Slowly, very slowly, Quincy pulled the curtain all the way back and climbed inside the tub, pulling his knees up to his chest, leaning his back against the rear. His eyes darting about wildly, he reached out with a shuddering hand and drew the curtain, so that he was completely enveloped, wholly protected by its defenses.

There now. There.

He took another deep breath, closing his eyes again. This time he pictured a city far away, some sprawling metropolis with towering skyscrapers and bustling streets and all-night restaurants, longing to be a part of it all, of the ceaseless excitement. Hadn't he once been perfectly capable of such? Hadn't he once been free to partake in precisely such revelry? And yet here was now, hiding and shivering in some cramped bathtub, with the curtain drawn, the thought of even opening the front door far too much to withstand.

It's better in here than out there. It's better in here than anywhere.

But it was a lie, and he knew it was a lie. He began to weep, to thrash about. He thought he might be choking. He thought his throat might be closing up. His heart galloped in his chest, the cords in his neck standing out, veins in his forehead bulging. He was paper-white, drenched in sweat, tensed into an awkward ball. He had to get out of there. He had to get to somewhere safer, somewhere smaller.

But there was nowhere smaller to go.

So pry up the floorboards.

The thought was absurd. The thought was insane.

There's a crowbar in the garage.

Suddenly, Quincy began to laugh. It was a wretched, bewildered sound, full of horror and revulsion. It went on for almost a full minute. When it finally died, Quincy reached out and grabbed the shower curtain and ripped it off the rod. He began to gnaw on it, the curtain, his legs now shaking so badly they beat against the sides of the tub like steel fists.

There's a crowbar in the garage.

"Leave me alone!" he shrieked. "Just leave me the hell *alone*! Just leave me alone, please. Please. *Please* leave me alone."

Pry up the floorboards. Now.

He laughed again, crying, and stuffed more of the curtain into his mouth. He chewed it slowly as he wept.

Outside, a neighbor pulled into her driveway, got out of her car, and looked at her lawn, wondering when it might snow.

FALLING LEAVES

It had been a long time coming. When the gates finally opened, Douglas stepped out calmly but warily, glancing back at the guards for a moment, and then out at the great wide open before him. He looked up at the sky and saw the sun sinking behind the mountains. It was the first sunset he'd seen in twelve years.

He boarded a bus, a bus bound for a city from which he had been long estranged. Things had changed, naturally. Old buildings had been torn down and new ones erected. Streets had been re-paved, potholes filled in. Billboards advertised products he'd never heard of. And the music on the radio was utterly foreign to him.

When the bus finally pulled into the station, Douglas waited for everyone else to get off, then stood with his single suitcase in his hand.

"Getting off?" asked the bus driver.

"Yes, sir," he said quietly, and moved toward the door.

"Have a nice evening."

"You too."

He stepped out, onto the ground, hallowed ground so far as *he* was concerned, and sat down for a moment on his suitcase. The desire for a cigarette overwhelmed him. The desire for a drink was quieter, more muted, but there, nagging gently at him. He would have both in due time.

But for now he was content to watch the sun set, to watch the sky darken piecemeal. He was content to watch the stars come out, twinkling dimly at first and then flaring in the night sky. Douglas breathed deeply of the air, savoring the freshness of it, the purity. It had been an eternity since he had last breathed open air.

Eventually he rose and took his suitcase in his hand and began walking toward his new home. It would be a small place, cold and beat-up and decrepit, but it would do. He would have his own place at last. He would be able to be alone. He wouldn't take that for granted.

When he got there the landlady was asleep. He woke her up by ringing the bell. She came to the door groggily, out of sorts, and asked him his name.

"Douglas Albright," he said.

She nodded and let him in, led him up to his room. It was indeed small, and sparsely furnished, but there was nice-sized bed and a lamp to read by. He had two books in his suitcase, and relished the thought of curling up in the bed and reading in total peace and quiet.

"Your room," she said.

"Thanks."

She closed the door behind her and he moved to the bed and sat down. He looked around. This was his new home, at least for now. And he could live with it. He could live with it gladly.

Douglas lay on the bed and looked out the window, at the leaves falling to the ground. It was autumn and the air was brisk. There was no heater in the room, and he could feel a cool draft seeping in through tears in the insulation around the window. His book lay supine on his chest. He had tried to read but couldn't focus. The leaves had kept distracting him.

That he had a view at all was incredible. That it was his and his alone seemed impossible. And it was a fine view, overlooking the park across the street and the beautiful elms that grew alongside the gate. He had played in the park as a child.

He would start work tomorrow, rebuilding engines at a local mechanic's shop. The parole board had set him up with the job. He was grateful for the opportunity, thought it kind of the mechanic to cut an ex-con a break. He had worked on engines as a teenager, in his uncle's garage. His uncle was dead now, stricken by a heart attack three years ago. But Douglas was also frightened. It had been a long time since such responsibility had been entrusted to him. He was scared of screwing up.

He tried again to read his book, got through a page and a half, and set it down again, set it aside. He stood and went to the window and opened it. He sat down and looked across the street to the park. There were three boys playing soccer under a floodlight, the ball kicking up brightly colored leaves, their shadows dancing on the short grass. They were laughing and jabbering, carrying on. They were happy.

A woman pushed a baby in a stroller along the sidewalk, lit faintly by orange sodium streetlamps. The canopy on the stroller was pulled over, the squeak of the wheels barely audible over the boys' laughter. The woman wore a long pink dress and white gloves and a red pillbox hat. She was like a character out of an old movie. Douglas smiled.

After some time he closed the window and returned to his bed. He opened his book and then closed it again. *Freedom,* he thought. It was a strange concept, one he had once understood perfectly well but now found opaque and elusive, even a little unseemly. There was a certain coarseness to it, a kind of dim vulgarity. It was oddly shaped and rough around the edges. What to do with it, with freedom itself? Where to go, whom to see? And what sense did it make that he should decide when to wake, when to eat, when to sleep again? It was a strange concept, indeed.

He undressed now and turned off the lamp and got into bed, rolled onto his side. He would start work tomorrow, and then maybe he would have a routine again. That would be nice. That would settle him a bit, he hoped. And after work he would eat dinner in his room, alone, where he was comfortable. He would read more of his book. He would smoke a cigarette and drink a beer.

Freedom, he thought. He thought of the boys playing soccer, how they had laughed and chattered wildly with the exuberance of youth. He thought of the woman pushing the stroller, how young she must have been, likely on her way home to see her new husband.

He thought of the leaves falling to the ground, how many colors they were, how beautiful they were. He thought he could make sense of freedom again, in time. He thought things would be all right.

He slept and dreamt of the cell he had slept in the night before, and when he woke the next day, he found himself lying at the foot of the bed, hands balled up into fists, back stiff as a board.

ITALIAN LOBSTER

Jimmy Simmons sat in a red vinyl booth, his eyes flitting back and forth between the window and the menu in his hands. The menu was the same laminated rectangle one finds in any roadside diner, announcing the same basic fare for offer: cheeseburgers, French fries, turkey sandwiches, hot wings, and chicken salads. None of it much appealed to him. He was distracted. He kept waiting for her car to pull up, the little red Chevy Cobalt she drove. He had a lot to tell her.

He'd met her at a car show the month before, and things had progressed quickly. They'd slept together the same night, and begun dating the day after. She had seemed to be everything he'd ever wanted in a woman: smart, funny, pretty, spontaneous. But then the inevitable had happened. He'd seen other sides of her, darker sides. Sides that frightened him. It was time, he thought, to break it off. And he wanted to do it on *his* terms, before she'd have a chance to do it on hers. Hers might be ugly.

"Sir?" He looked up and saw a lanky waitress standing over him, her lean face bearing a constellation of whiteheads, a blue Bic pen in her right hand and a notepad in her left. She looked to be in her late twenties or early thirties, rather too old to be afflicted with acne. A splotch of mustard was encrusting itself to her apron. "Are you ready to order?"

"Um," he said. "Maybe just a few more minutes?"

"Take all the time you need, sir."

"Thank you."

He looked out the window again. Still nothing. The sky was gray, probably heralding snow. The temperature outside had been dropping quickly.

He glanced around the diner, saw a big man clad in a plaid flannel shirt and grimy jeans (a trucker, Jimmy figured) sipping coffee at the counter. A teenage boy with a scar on his forehead occupied another of the booths, fiddling with a rubber band over a half-eaten hot dog. An old woman was noshing on a dinner roll at one of the tables. The tables were round with red-and-white checkered cloths draped over them. Fifties paraphernalia decorated the walls, records and pennants and photographs of celebrities, most of them black-and-white. The wall above the counter was a bastion of mostly southern-flavored Americana, a Route 66 sign and bumper stickers ("Freedom Isn't Free," "Rebel Rider," "American by Birth, Southern by the grace of God") pasted between a Gadsen flag on one end and a Confederate flag on the other. All standard trimmings, Jimmy supposed, for a diner in rural Alabama.

He stood up on watery legs and headed for the bathroom. Traci was obviously going to make him wait. In the meantime he'd relieve himself and get himself centered. It wasn't going to be easy or pleasant, what was about to transpire. He needed to be steady.

The bathroom was all that he'd expected: a single toilet with a shit-stained seat, corroded stall door loose on its hinges; a near-empty roll of ultra-thin toilet paper hanging on crooked brackets; a damp floor with buckled tiles; and a streaky, dimly lit mirror over a cracked porcelain sink sprouting hairs of dubious origin from its drain. The light was yellow, sickly. Jimmy's reflection looked drawn and pallid and unwell. He turned his eyes away from the mirror and moved to the toilet.

She'd better have a damned good reason, he thought as he unbuckled his belt, *for being late.*

He'd barely sat down again before the waitress was back, her notepad now in her left hand instead of her right. "Ready to order, sir?"

"I think I'll just have a plain burger with ketchup and mustard."

"No cheese?" she asked, frowning. She seemed almost offended.

"No, thanks."

"Or lettuce or pickles?"

"Just plain," he said firmly. "Thank you."

"No problem, sir. If I can take that menu off your hands?"

"Sure." He handed her the plastic rectangle and shifted his eyes back to the window. It was almost dark now.

"Our special is Italian Lobster," she said.

Jimmy turned back to her. "I'm sorry?"

"Italian Lobster," she repeated. "It's our special. And it's *excellent*." She spoke with a thick southern drawl, dragging her words out. She gave a slight, lop-sided, somehow unnerving smile, revealing an incomplete set of stained, crooked teeth. Jimmy noticed for the first time just how *greasy* her hair looked, how unkempt.

"I don't know what Italian lobster is," he said. "But just the hamburger will be -"

"It's lobsters from *Italy*," she declared loudly. "They swim off the coast of *Italy*. They's the best lobsters in the whole wide *world!*"

"Really?" Jimmy said. He swallowed. "I didn't realize Italy was famous for its lobsters. And I'm rather surprised such a... humble diner as this would serve so prized a commodity."

She blinked at him rapidly, then smiled again. A shiver went down his spine. "We have 'em flowed over special, from Sicily." She pronounced this last word *Seesalee*.

"That's something." His tone was even and accommodating, but inwardly he was a bit perturbed now. There was something wrong here, clearly, and not just with the waitress. There was something wrong with the diner itself. Suddenly all he wanted was to stand up and walk out. But Traci –

"I'll get your burger," said the waitress, and all at once he felt almost okay again, told himself he was just overreacting to an eccentric personality.

The waitress turned and headed for the kitchen. Jimmy looked out the window again. A light snow had begun to fall, wet flakes swirling in the dusty lamplight of the parking lot. Still there was no sign of Traci.

Jimmy lit a cigarette and ran his hand through his hair. Was she doing this on purpose? Was she playing games? He drummed his fingers on the table for a moment, then took out his cell phone and pulled up her last text, sent two days ago: "Phone being turned off 2morrow. Should be back on by Fri. See you at diner Thurs at 7." He closed his phone and put it back in his pocket, stubbing out his cigarette in a foil ashtray.

"Your lobster, sir," said the waitress. She was standing over him again, holding a big silver tray with a lid over it, like the sort that Sylvester the Cat salivated over in the *Looney Tune* cartoons when he thought Tweety Bird was trapped inside. Except, when Sylvester lifted the lid, there was no trace of the bird save a stray feather.

"I didn't order -" Jimmy began.

Then the waitress lifted the lid, revealing a live lobster perched on a cafeteria-white plate. Its pinchers were slowly opening and closing, its antennae probing the air as the crustacean itself slowly suffocated. The waitress was beaming proudly.

"What the hell's going on here?" he demanded now. His heart had sped up a little. A light sweat glistened on his brow.

"It's the lobster you ordered, sir. The Italian Lobster." Her accent was somehow even thicker than before.

"That's a live goddam lobster!"

"Eat it," the waitress said, suddenly grabbing the plate and dumping the grasping red fiend into Jimmy's lap. "Eat the lobster!"

"Jesus Christ!" He stood and let the anthropod fall to the floor. Its pinchers suddenly clasped his pant leg and dug into his skin. He yelped and kicked it off.

"Why would you waste *food* like that?" the waitress asked him. She grimaced, as if putting up with a rude customer. "He's from *Italy!*"

"There's no such thing as a fucking... Italian *lobster!*"

"God*dammit!*" she yelled. She started ripping up the sheets on her notepad and throwing the shreds into the air like confetti. She poked him gently in the arm with her pen. "You are being *awful*. Our other specials include the Glazed Wheat of Lamb, Sautéed Carrots and Pie, Scandinavian maca-*rooooons*, and BELGIAN HAMHOCKS!"

"That's just gibberish." His voice was still calm, but his heart was now thudding like a trip-hammer. He shot a discreet glance at the door on the other side of the diner, scared to fully break eye contact with the waitress, scared of what she might do if he did. Meanwhile, the lobster writhed helplessly on the floor under the table, one of its pinchers having fallen still, the other yawning in a death throe.

"It is *not!*" she barked. "Is not, is not, is NOT!"

"I'll be leaving now."

He turned away, ready to make a bee-line for the door, when he felt a terrible stabbing pain in his rib cage. The pain fanned upward, into his shoulder and neck, virtually paralyzing him. He looked down and saw that the waitress had skewered him with her pen. It was jutting out of his side like an arrow, blood dribbling down his shirt.

"You *bitch!*" he cried, yanking the pen free. "What the fuck is *wrong* with you? I'll be calling -"

"*Bitch!*" she yelled back, slapping him across the face with the back of her bony hand. "*You're* a bitch! *You* are! Now get down on your hands and knees and eat that fucking Italian Lobster, you little *bitch!* They flowed it here just for *you!*" She slapped him again, this time with her palm, whipping his face the other way.

Now he grabbed her, forcefully, and pushed her ten yards across the floor, into the counter. Plates and cutlery crashed over the edge and shattered, clattered upon the floor. He reached for her hair, pulled on it, and she bit him on the hand, sinking her teeth deep into his flesh, almost to the bone. He let out a terrific wail. "Mmmm!" she cried. "You taste like a lightly braised pork *sammich!*"

"You're crazy," he said, still restraining her by her arms. She spat in his face, then burst out laughing. It was a wild, rambling, high-pitched laugh, brimming over with lunacy. Her eyes gleamed madly in the waxy, artificial light of the diner.

"Yup," she said, licking her lips. "But guess what?"

He gave her another shove. Another plate crashed upon the floor. "What?"

"Your little girlfriend's *dead*. Yeah. She *died* on her way here."

"What the fuck are you talking about?"

The waitress guffawed again. "Ha! Ha! Ha! She's *deaaaaaaad.*"

"What's her name? Huh? Tell me her name."

The waitress bit her bottom lip, eyes rolled up in their sockets, the pupils barely visible. She looked like an epileptic at the end of a bad seizure. "Traaaaaci."

"You *bitch*," Jimmy snarled, and shook her. That's when the cook emerged from the kitchen, a brawny man in a white short-order chef's hat and an apron splattered with various stains. He sported a week's worth of stubble on his chin and neck. Tattoos ran the lengths of his arms. His chest heaved as he stood anxiously in the doorway, hands balled into fists.

Slowly, Jimmy released the waitress, who now giggled and darted into the kitchen. He groaned and felt the wound in his side, blood caking on his shirttail. As if waking from a dream, he surveyed the diner, saw that the other patrons were still exactly where they had been, still doing exactly as they'd been doing: the fat trucker was still sitting at the end of the counter, sipping his coffee; the old lady was still taking dainty bites of her dinner roll, hardly any smaller; and the teenage boy was still in the booth, playing with his rubber band. Jimmy looked at him for a moment, watched as he pulled the rubber band as far apart as it would stretch before letting it snap back against his fingers. The kid laughed dumbly and did it again.

"Did you have a problem with the lobster I made for you?" the cook asked sulkily, his voice that of a scolded child. His eyes were big and absurdly sad. His bottom lip quivered. He looked like a man on the brink of a nervous breakdown, or murder.

"No," Jimmy said, backing toward the door. "I didn't. I'm just... not very hungry right now."

"That's too bad," the cook said, producing a large butcher knife from behind his back. He ran his finger gently along the blade, a long blade which glinted sickeningly in the wan light. "I worked real hard on it, too. Cooked it juuuuust *right*."

51

It's still alive, Jimmy thought. Only it wasn't, as a quick glance under his table confirmed.

He looked back at the cook, who took a step forward. Jimmy, accordingly, took a step backward. Out the corner of his eye, he saw the portly trucker push his coffee aside and draw a handgun from his waistband. He turned and watched as the old lady dropped her dinner roll on the floor, removed her dentures, and submerged them in her glass of milk. And then, abruptly, the teenage boy tapped him on the shoulder.

He turned with a start, eyes wide and staring, and saw to his horror that the boy was holding a small tomahawk in his right hand. "Say, Mister," said the boy. The word came out *Meeester*. His shirt accentuated his bulging biceps. His jeans were tight-fitting and dusty. His skin was sallow, eyes sleepy and vacant. "You didn't finish yer *lobster*."

"I... I was going to," Jimmy stammered.

The boy raised his tomahawk to his mouth, ran the blade along his lip. "Then why *didn'tcha*?"

Jimmy tried to swallow but couldn't. His mouth was bone-dry. "I, uh... I just..." He turned, meaning to dash into the bathroom, and bumped directly into the cook, who turned him back around to face the boy again.

"You just... *what?*"

"Didn't get a chance."

"Well," said the boy. "We'll give you another." He looked at the cook. "Won't we, Dick?"

"Sure," said the cook. His voice had lost all of its plaintive quality, was now purely sinister. "Sure we will."

"So get over there and eat that fuckin' lobster!" the boy screamed. "On your hands and knees, just like Gladys told you to!"

"Start with the eye," Dick said gloomily. "The eye's the best part."

"It's true," chirped the old lady. She went over to the booth where Jimmy had sat, bent down, and retrieved the now-defunct lobster. She carried it over to him and lifted it to his mouth. "The eyes is just so, sooooo good."

A car pulled up outside, obscured by darkness and snow. But it *sounded* like Traci's, had the same basic *shape* as Traci's. If he could just –

"*Eat* it!" the old bat screamed shrilly. "Eat that gooey Iiiii-talian eye!"

"Eat it or take a goddamned bullet to your head, son." Jimmy felt a muzzle press against the back of his head, heard a faint *click*. "That's your choice." He could feel the trucker's foul hot breath on the back of his neck.

"I'll eat it," Jimmy said. "I will. Just let me -"

"Eat!"

A car door opened, closed. A shadowy figure approached the diner. Shaking violently, Jimmy took a tiny bite of the lobster's eye. It was mushy and coppery on his tongue. Fluid burst from it as he bit down. He thought he might vomit.

The door opened. "Jimmy?" Traci's voice. Thank God. He was saved. "What the hell -"

The trucker turned and fired three shots in rapid succession. Traci's body slumped to the floor, her nettlesome query promptly silenced. Jimmy cried out, tried to shake off his captors, but it was futile. They held him fast, completely surrounding him now, crowding into him.

"It's Iiiiii-talian," said the old lady.

"Eat one of the pinchers," said the cook.

"I'm gonna go see how your girlfriend's doing," said the boy. "My tomahawk needs sharpening."

Jimmy bit down on one of the lobster's pinchers. He retched, then barfed all over the cook's apron. The cook laughed and pulled Jimmy's head against his chest, smearing the vomit all over his face. The old lady went over to the windows and began closing the blinds.

From near the door, Jimmy heard the sound of a zipper coming undone.

And the cook sang, in a perfect tenor's voice, "Let it snow, let it snow, let it snow!"

A PORCH PAINTED WHITE

Every day Evan drove by the house, the old house with battered aluminum siding and crooked shutters. He knew it was the only thing Jason owned outright, maybe the only thing the boy would *ever* own outright. His car was a loaner. His furniture was rented. The house he'd inherited from an aunt. He might have had sixty dollars to his name, but Evan knew he'd still put a dollar in the basket at tonight's meeting. He always did.

Winter was moving in. The air had grown crisp and chilly, the trees all but barren. Today Jason was dressed in raggedy blue jeans and a black hoodie over a white t-shirt. His hair was tousled, his face unshaven. His eyes looked bloodshot, but Evan knew it wasn't from drink. It was from lack of sleep.

He pulled his truck into the driveway and got out. He approached the porch slowly, lowering his head against the wind. Jason was painting one of the posts and now looked up and dropped the brush into the paint can. He was covered in white splotches.

"Evan," he said. His voice was hoarse, probably from too much smoking, and he cleared his throat. "I didn't expect you so early."

"I had a free hour," Evan said. "Thought I'd stop by and check on you. How's the porch coming?"

Jason nodded languidly. "It's coming."

"It looks good." Evan reached into his pocket and brought out a pack of Malboros. "Smoke?"

"Thanks," Jason said, sliding a cigarette out of the pack.

"Here you go." Evan produced a lighter and lit Jason's cigarette, then lit one of his own. He inhaled deeply, appraising the porch. "How much longer, do you think?"

"Maybe a day or two."

Evan nodded. "And what then?"

Jason shrugged. "I don't know. I reckon I'll find something else to paint. Something else to do."

Evan nodded again, pointing to one of the rocking chairs on the porch. "Do you mind?"

Jason shrugged. "Whatever you want."

Evan sat with a sigh, taking another drag on his cigarette. He looked out at the potholed road, the littered ditches, the ramshackle houses caving in on themselves. He looked beyond, to the sprawling field full of dandelions and dead grass and cattails swaying in the autumn breeze at the bank of the pond, and at the gray clouds overhead. He turned up the collar of his coat and wrapped his arms around his middle. "How have you been, Jason?"

"I been okay."

"Do you mean that?"

Jason looked at him, his face strained and red from the cold. "Yeah, I mean that."

"Any luck finding work?"

"Not so far."

"I know you liked being a cook."

Jason frowned. "I'd rather not..." He trailed off, sighed. "I'd rather not talk about it, if it's all the same to you."

Evan nodded and licked his chapped lips. "I didn't mean to upset you."

"You didn't upset me. I just don't... you know."

Evan looked at him. "Want to talk about your past?"

"Yeah. That."

"I understand."

Jason grimaced and smoked, looked down at the paint can as if wishing he could get back to work.

"Let's talk about your future, then."

"I'd just as soon not discuss that, either."

Evan contorted his face, thinking. A long moment passed. "Are you working your Steps?"

"Yes."

"Are you still... you know?"

Jason looked at him with hard but hazy eyes, sniffling. A string of clear snot was drying on the right sleeve of his hoodie. "Am I still what? Sad? Depressed?"

"Haunted by what happened to you," Evan said, brushing off the coal of his cigarette with the hard, mud-caked sole of his steel-toe boot. He put the butt into his coat pocket.

"Of course I am. Every day. Every day I wake up and live with it. Every day I have to face it. I didn't do a goddam thing wrong, and here I am, with no job and no... no wife. Here I am –"

"Just take it easy, Jason."

"Here I am, painting a goddam porch fence I don't even care about! And Jesus, Evan... I mean..."

Evan had been rocking in the chair and now brought it still. He looked Jason in the eye, intently. "I only came here to help you," he said. "I only came here to talk."

"What's there to talk about? My sobriety? Whether I'm working the Steps? My goddam... *future*?"

"Well," Evan said awkwardly, "yes."

"It's bullshit," Jason said. "All of it."

"Hey, now."

"Maybe you should go. I know you're my sponsor and all, but –"

"I'll go if that's what you want."

"It is."

Evan nodded, clamping a hand around his neck. "Then I'll go. But can I check on you tomorrow?"

Jason shrugged. "You'll see me tonight, won't you?"

"I don't know," Evan said. "Will I?"

Jason nodded vaguely, stood up, and went inside. Evan sat for a moment longer, then rose and peered through the window in the door. Jason was nowhere to be seen. "Okay," Evan said quietly. "All right." He plodded down the steps and got into his truck and drove off, a heavy sense of dread bearing down on him.

Much as Evan had feared, Jason hadn't shown up for the meeting the night before. Evan had waited outside the church for a good ten minutes afterwards, smoking and thinking vain thoughts and resenting the cold. Eventually he'd gone home, and tried calling, but there had been no answer. Just the machine with a banal outgoing message. Evan had hung up without saying a word.

Now he drove to the house, the old house with the battered aluminum siding and crooked shutters. He grew increasingly antsy along the way, shifting about in his seat, wiping sweat from his brow. His heart was beating too fast and his palms were slick and his mind had begun to race with unpalatable thoughts. He had not felt so nervous in years.

When he got to the house he pulled into the driveway and splashed his truck's headlights over the porch fence. The paintjob was finished, the posts and rails a pristine, uniform white. They looked brand-new.

Evan cut the engine and got out. The wind stabbed at his face and he pulled his fur-lined hood over his head and made his way toward the steps. Then he stopped, turned around.

The houses across the street were quiet and dark. The lawns, craggy and unkempt, passed muster in the faint moonlight. And the field and pond were all but invisible, silent but for the distant croaking of restless frogs. Evan might have been in a perfectly lovely suburban neighborhood just then, might have been standing in the driveway of his own boyhood home.

He looked at Jason's house, perfectly still and dark but for a lone bulb shining over the porch. He took a step forward, stopped, and bit his lower lip. The cold was terrible, seizing him like a nasty fist. He tried to take another step toward the porch but couldn't. He lowered his head and turned around and went back to his truck.

He got into the driver's seat and started the engine and turned on the headlights. He pressed his hand to the horn, letting it blat just for a moment, and then jerked it away, as if from a hot coal. He waited. He waited a full minute. But nobody stirred, and there was no noise but that of the howling wind.

He backed down the driveway slowly, looking at the porch again, and as he pulled onto the road he thought, *At least you finished what you started.*

A WINTER EVENING BY THE LAKE

The sun was coming down and we parked the car near the drop-off and left the engine running for the heat. A cloud of dust settled behind us, collecting on the rear window, clinging to the tires and bumper. Tall trees surrounded us on either side, mammoth elms and stout pines vanishing into a gray sky that threatened snow. Their branches were nearly bare now, like arms bereft of sleeves, trembling slightly in the cold gusts that blew through. The last of their leaves fluttered down onto the hood of our car, and the windshield, and I remember being overcome by sadness and grief at the sight of them. They were brown, fragile, melancholy things, deprived of will, swirling about aimlessly in a blind zephyr. I could relate to them.

It was the brink of winter and, for us, the beginning of the end. It was a time of terrific hesitation and vast uncertainty, of creeping doubts and awkward silences. If going back is impossible, then there are moments when going forward can be so daunting that it, too, had might as well be. These are moments of perfect paralysis, moments when movement in any direction spawns mighty dread. Yet the stillness is no better, no more comfortable. The stillness stings, a constant reminder that while inertia might be safe, it can resolve nothing.

I turned the heat up and glanced over at Julie. She was rubbing her hands together in front of one of the vents, her head lowered. She was frowning.

"We'll be all right," I said. I didn't believe it.

"I remember," she said, "when we were first married. I remember -"

But I wanted to hear none of that. "Things happen," I said. "People change."

"Which of us changed, though?"

Both, was the easy answer. But it wasn't true. "I did."

"We came here every summer."

"And now we're here at the start of winter."

"We made love under those trees."

"Julie."

She looked up at me, her face drawn, lips pressed tightly together. There were tears in her eyes. "I still love you, John."

I sighed and turned on the radio. "There's a sandwich in the glove box if you're hungry."

"What did we come out here for?"

"To say good-bye," I said. "Just like you wanted."

But it wasn't what she'd really wanted and we seldom say what we really want and we seldom do what we mean to. I'd discovered all that in the past few months. I'd discovered that since she'd asked for a divorce. She wouldn't eat the sandwich, I knew. It was peanut butter and banana, her favorite, but she wouldn't eat it. I'd known she wouldn't eat it when I'd made it. I'd probably eat it later myself.

"Do you want to talk?" she asked.

Our lives had been good, for the most part. We hadn't had much money, but we'd had enough. We'd both had jobs we could tolerate. There was talk of children but it never came to pass. And at nighttime we usually made love, sometimes with passion and sometimes routinely, sometimes just to pass the time, to make ourselves sleepy. Julie had always had more trouble sleeping than I had. Women's minds never quit.

"What's there to talk about?" I asked.

"Us," she said.

"We're over." I looked at her. "Aren't we?"

"Yes, but -" She cut herself off abruptly. Yes but what? But we could still be friends? But the time we'd spent together had not been in vain? That she didn't regret a day of it? None of it was true, and Julie wasn't one to fib.

"I came out here to say good-bye," I said. "And to see the lake one last time."

"It's frozen over."

"It's nice."

Now she put her hand on my leg, and I brushed it off. I'd become distant, she'd said. She was right. I had. It turns out we become at least as distant from others as we become from ourselves, and I hadn't seen myself, really seen myself, in ages.

"What's nice about it?" she asked.

"It's peaceful. Calm."

I imagined skating on that ice, although I couldn't skate, and imagined fishing through a hole in it, though I didn't fish. My imagination was a fertile thing far more capable than I. It was fun to indulge.

"I wish it were summertime," she said. "I wish the sun would come out and thaw the lake so we could go swimming."

"We never swam in the lake." Her imagination was perhaps even more fertile than mine.

"We should have."

I should have married someone else, I thought. *Or no one at all.* And probably the latter was closer to the truth. Maybe I wasn't meant to be with anyone for too long. I'd never had trouble falling in love with a woman, but I'd always had trouble *staying* in love with one. Maybe it was impossible for me to love anyone for long, or to truly love anyone at all.

"I don't like to swim," I said.

"I do."

"You don't want your sandwich?"

"No."

"I'll have it later, then."

Everything had been later, always. Everything would happen later, come true later, be okay later. Tomorrow had been, always, as magical as today was disappointing. Tomorrow would cure everything. Only tomorrow had proved elusive, and today decisive: some things just couldn't be put off forever.

"I remember when we met," Julie said.

"So do I."

"I thought you were so handsome."

"If only that was enough."

"You thought I was beautiful. Didn't you?"

"I did."

A tear now spilled down her cheek. It wasn't a momentous thing, at least not to me; it was more like a small sneeze. "Things never work out, do they, John?"

"I reckon sometimes they do. Just not always when or how they should."

"Things always work out wrong."

"For us, maybe."

She wiped the tear from her cheek, cast a glance out the window. "Who else is there?"

I looked at her, smiled faintly. "Babe," I said, "we were only as special as we thought we were."

The sun was almost fully set now, dead leaves still dancing in the wind, mustard-colored grass stirring between the rocks and the trees. I looked out at the lake, a round sheet of craggy ice, barren save for a lone cardinal flitting from spot to spot. It was a bowl in the earth, a perfect depression, a serene thing which knew no strife. It just was what it was, and that was all.

I turned to Julie. "We should get going," I said.

"Okay."

I put the car in reverse and backed up. Turning around, I glanced at the frozen lake, now almost fully obscured by darkness, in the rearview mirror. Sometimes we just have to leave things behind, I realized. Sometimes things belong to the past all along.

THE GOOD CHRISTIANS' CLUB

Linda had borrowed her husband's truck, just to run an errand. She'd gone to the post office to mail a package to her sister-in-law. It was Christmas presents, an old-fashioned snow globe featuring the baby Jesus and the Magi, and a stuffed, frost-bitten Santa hauling a sack of gifts over his shoulder. Linda knew her sister-in-law would especially appreciate the snow globe: Linda was a devout Christian, had a picture of Jesus in nearly every room of her house, and a Bible in every bedroom drawer. The Santa might not go over so well, but so be it. Linda enjoyed the secular aspects of Christmas as much as the religious, and she'd be damned if Alice wouldn't learn to do the same.

Linda had taken her husband's truck because the forecast had called for heavy snow and the truck had much better traction than her little Honda. She'd begun to doubt the forecast on her way to the post office, the sun still shining brightly and not so much as a flurry in the air. But by the time she'd walked out the sun had disappeared and gray clouds loomed on the horizon. A few minutes into her journey home, the snow had started to fall, sticking to the road immediately. The temperature had dropped ten degrees in an hour. The streets, still damp from a morning shower, froze over almost instantly.

She began to worry when the truck skidded a bit around a curve. She began to worry more when the snow started falling so heavily and suddenly that she was forced to put her wipers on the fastest speed and could barely see more than five feet in front of her face. Her fingers bore down on the wheel, her knuckles turning paper-white. Her lips pursed themselves into a small, twitching oval. Her mouth went dry, making it hard to swallow. That's when she remembered the bottle of water in her handbag.

She reached over for it, keeping her eyes on the road and her other hand planted firmly on the wheel. She fumbled about in her bag, feeling her purse and pens and candy wrappers but no bottle of water. Frustrated, she looked over at the passenger's seat, down at her bag, and dug deeper, finally wrapping her hand around the top of the bottle.

You've got to be careful, she thought. *This truck isn't insured yet.*

When she looked up again, she was barreling toward an SUV with flaring brake lights, and instinctively slammed her foot down on her own brake pedal. She heard the tires spin briefly on the slick road, and then lock. The vehicle catapulted forward, sliding uncontrollably down a steep hill at a sharp angle. She turned into the skid, as her husband had always told her to do, but it was useless. The front end of the Chevy pickup rammed the back end of the blue Subaru Forester at about twenty miles per hour, deploying the truck's air bag and slinging the truck into a deep, narrow ditch at the side of the road. The big SUV had deflected the small truck like a wayward pinball.

The truck tipped to the right, bounced back to the left, and finally fell still. Linda was jostled about but restrained by her seatbelt and the air bag. Gasping, shaking, she turned to look out the window and saw nothing but swirling snow, the road buried under a thin blanket of white spoiled only by two erratic, snaking grooves, the marks left by the truck's tires. Her hands trembling badly, she put her shoulder against the driver's-side door and muscled it open.

She crawled out on all fours, nearly collapsing to the ground, scraping the palms of her hands on gravel and twigs. The cold hit her hard, a strong gust of wind blasting her face and making her eyes water. Snow stung her nose and cheeks and the back of her neck, melting on her skin so that trickles of water seeped under the collar of her coat. She shivered, and looked toward the mangled Subaru Forester. The snow was all but blinding, but Linda could see the steady strobe of the car's hazard lights, bright orange pulses in gray-white air.

She got to her feet and tottered toward the SUV. The driver got out, a petite blonde woman with perfect skin and crimson cheeks and eyes like the ice on the road: hard, flinty, and such a pale blue that they were almost translucent. She trudged carefully up the hill, minding her every step, approaching Linda with a pained but seemingly authentic smile. And now her eyes softened, too.

"Are you okay?" she asked.

"I'm... fine, I think. What about you?"

The woman reached up and rubbed her neck with a pink wool mitten. "My neck hurts a little," she said. "I might have whiplash. But otherwise I feel all right."

"I'm so sorry." The two women had finally reached each other, nebulous shapes shuddering in a blizzard. "Should we call for an ambulance?"

The blonde woman smiled demurely. "I don't think that's necessary."

Linda extended a bare hand, already raw and chapped from the cold. "I'm Linda Silkowski."

"Mary Anne Magdalene." The woman's handshake was assertive but gentle.

"Like the Mary in the Bible?" Linda asked, trying to smile but too damned cold to quite manage it.

"That's right," said Mary Anne. "Should we exchange phone numbers? I think my car is still drivable. Is yours?"

"I don't know. I'm sort of stuck in the ditch." Linda gestured, and Mary Anne's eyes followed. "I may need a tow truck. But listen -"

"I have a cell phone. Let me call one for you."

"It's okay," said Linda. "I have a cell phone, too. But I'm afraid what I *don't* have is car insurance."

Mary Anne's face dropped, almost comically. "Oh."

"I know it sounds awful and all. I mean, I know it's illegal not to have it, but my husband and I just bought the truck, and we just hadn't gotten around to insuring it yet. But I'd be happy to -"

Mary Anne put her hand on Linda's arm, squeezing it tightly. "I don't want you to worry about this," she said. "I think we both just need to get out of the cold and let the traffic through."

"Okay."

"And I know you probably can't afford to pay for the damage out-of-pocket," Mary Anne continued. "So I won't ask you to."

Linda shook her head, insistent. Her legs were starting to go numb. "But the accident was my fault."

"It doesn't matter," said Mary Anne. "You couldn't help what happened, I'm sure. So I forgive you for it. But there is *one* thing I'd ask you to do, just as a token of goodwill."

Linda nodded. "Okay. What is it?"

"Here," Mary Anne said, producing what appeared to be a business card from her jacket pocket.

"What's this? Your phone number?"

"Look at it."

So Linda looked at it, trying to decipher the words on it as best she could in the crossing gusts of snow. The card was egg-shell white with raised black font, quite professional-looking. It said:

The Good Christians' Club

Meetings Every Wed. & Sat. Nite

@ 7 p.m.

COME ONE, COME ALL!

"I don't understand," Linda said. "Do you want me to come to one of your meetings?"

"No," said Mary Anne. "I don't *want* you to, Linda. I *expect* you to." She smiled then, and the smile was really no less genuine than that with which the woman had first greeted her. But something about it made Linda rather uneasy, and all of a sudden all she wanted was to be back home with Billy, with her husband, snuggling up by the fireplace.

"I'll try my best," Linda said in a small, quiet voice.

Mary Anne's smile did not falter. "So I'll see you on Saturday night, then?"

Linda nodded and mustered a smile of her own. "You bet."

"She doesn't even know our address," Billy said, exasperated. He forked a few peas and stuffed them into his mouth. "So why bother?"

"Because I said I would." Her own meal had gone largely untouched.

"So?" Billy looked at her over another forkful of peas. He'd already devoured his steak.

"So I keep my promises," she said. "Or at least try to. Besides, I'm kind of curious to see what it's all about."

Billy laughed, now digging into his mashed potatoes. "It's just gonna be a bunch of religious freaks."

"Maybe."

"Where is it?"

"First Church of Christ. The non-denominational on Second Street."

"On a Saturday night?"

"Yes. Every Wednesday and Saturday at seven p.m."

"Weird."

"Billy," she said, now rather annoyed herself. "I probably did a grand worth of damage to this woman's car. The least I can do is humor her for an hour or two. It's one night out of my life. And it's not like *you'd* be taking me anywhere, right?"

Billy sighed and dropped his fork on his plate, then wiped his mouth with his napkin. "Knock yourself out, sweetie. Just don't come home brainwashed like Alice, all right?" He stood and carried his plate to the sink – almost a first for him.

"Please," she said. She rose from the table, went to him, and wrapped her arms around his waist. She whispered in his ear: "How about I come home horny instead?"

He turned around, grinning. "I'll praise Jesus with you," he said, and kissed her.

The room was smaller than Linda had expected, and darker. Maroon curtains were drawn over casement windows, the carpet was a plum berber, and round plastic chairs the color of mustard were arranged in a tight circle. The only source of light was a dim florescent on the ceiling. Three women and two men stood around the circle of chairs, mingling and sipping punch out of frosted plastic cups. The punch bowl sat on a folding table in the far corner of the room, along with a coffee pot and a rack of literature. Linda was reminded, unpleasantly, of the A.A. meetings she'd been forced to attend in her early twenties to avoid jail time for a DUI.

She now walked nervously into the room, helped herself to a cup of black coffee. When she turned around, Mary Anne was standing in front of her, dressed in a yellow chiffon dress and platinum heels. Her face was impeccably made up, her lips a dark, ruby red, her eyelashes charcoal black, her hair tied in a tasteful bun. She might have been a Mary Kay model.

"Linda!" she cried excitedly. "I'm so glad you could make it!"

Linda forced a smile. "Of course. Wouldn't miss it. How's your car?"

"In the shop," said Mary Anne. "Being fixed. The damage was less than I thought it would be, actually."

"Oh, good. Are you absolutely sure -"

"Did you find the church okay?"

Linda fumbled for words, her heart fluttering a little in her chest. "Oh, sure. My husband and I have been here a few times before."

"Is that right? Are you Baptists?"

Linda renewed her smile. "We're... Christians. We've been to a lot of churches."

Mary Anne nodded, somewhat dreamily. She'd been beaming from the start, her eyes twinkling like the jewelry on her wrists. "That's good to hear, Linda. But I think after tonight you'll only want to come here."

Linda feigned consideration, and a thoughtful nod. "Maybe so. Maybe so."

Mary Anne just went on beaming, and looking at her, as if waiting for Linda to say something more.

"Can I... can I ask you something, Mary Anne?"

"Well, sure you can!"

"Okay. Well... what exactly *is* this?"

Mary Anne laughed, a bit unnervingly. "Why, it's a meeting for good Christians, silly!"

"Good Christians?"

"Like you and your husband. What's his name, by the way?"

"Um. Billy."

"I don't think I've met him."

"So is this... is this like a Bible study group, or...?"

"Oh, Linda," Mary Anne said. "You'll see!"

At that very moment, a loud, deep voice called the meeting to order. Everyone took a seat immediately, and the light dimmed further. Linda didn't see how that was possible, given that nobody had flipped a switch or turned a knob, but she was certain that the room got darker. Just a little, but definitely darker. Mary Anne guided her to a pair of empty chairs, almost pushing her into the one on her right. "Sit next to me," she said. "You'll be more comfortable that way."

There was a long moment of perfect silence, and then the man who had called the meeting to order –a tall, stocky fellow whom Linda presumed the leader of the group – lowered his head and intoned somberly from his seat: "Jesus Christ, Our Lord, may You bless us this night, this cold and holy night, as we gather here together, the Good Christians of Woodford County, to celebrate our faith in You and to testify to the strength and comfort it affords us. May You watch over us, and keep us safe, and fill our hearts with Your goodness and love, that we shall be reminded always of the sacrifice You made for us, the suffering You endured that we might attain Salvation, and know You eternally, in the wondrous bliss of Your Father's kingdom, Amen."

"Amen," replied the group in unison.

The tall, stocky man now raised his head and swept his eyes across his scant audience. "My name is Pastor Stephen Gibbons," he said. He was seated directly across from Linda, dressed in a burgundy cashmere sweater and tan slacks and a brown corduroy jacket with leather patches on the elbows. He reminded Linda of the professor who'd taught her Romantic Poets course her sophomore year of college. "I am the humble chairperson of the Woodford County chapter of the Good Christians' Club. I am honored to lead this group."

"Yes, Pastor," said one of the congregants, an elderly woman in a white cotton dress.

"Tonight's agenda is a busy one," continued the pastor. "We have a good many things to cover and discuss, such as Sunday's prayer breakfast at the Brickenstalt Hospice and next week's Christmas healing right here at First Church of Christ. But first, are there any newcomers to the group?"

Linda sat frozen in her seat. Mary Anne immediately turned to her, beaming again, and then looked at the pastor. "I'd like to introduce Linda Silkowski," Mary Anne said as if presenting a celebrity. "She and I met earlier this week under... well, rather unfortunate circumstances."

"Welcome, Linda!" trumpeted the group. Linda was again reminded, more vividly this time, of the A.A. meetings she'd once attended, of their cult-like atmosphere and unsettling homogeneity of thought.

"Thanks," Linda said sheepishly. "Good to be here."

"Where do you come from, Linda?" asked Pastor Gibbons.

"Right here in Woodford County."

"Strattonburg?"

"Uh huh."

Pastor Gibbons gave a strained smile, leaned forward a bit. "Here at the Woodford County Good Christians' Club, we say, 'Yes, Pastor.' It's a show of respect."

"Oh," said Linda, her mouth like a cotton ball. "I'm sorry. Yes, Pastor, I'm from Strattonburg."

"Well, that's just *lovely*. Isn't that lovely, folks?"

The group, in unison: "Yes, Pastor."

"Linda, why don't you tell us a little about yourself?"

"Yes, Linda," Mary Anne chimed in. "Tell us about yourself."

"Oh, gee," Linda said, blushing, "I'm sort of shy. I'd rather not."

The pastor grimaced. "You'd rather *not*?"

"Um. Oh, geez."

"Tell us about yourself," volunteered a young man in a suit and tie. His hair was combed meticulously, his legs crossed at the knee, as dapper and genteel as any man Linda had ever seen.

"Well, um... I was born in Missouri, in a little town called Bolivar. I'm the second of three children, two girls and one boy. I've been a certified nursing assistant for almost twelve years now, and -"

"Do you drink?" asked the pastor.

"I'm sorry?"

"Alcohol. Do you drink it?"

"I... I have a glass of wine every now and again. I'm sorry, I don't think I understand the point of your question?"

"What about drugs? Do you use them?"

"No. I don't. But what on earth -"

"'No, Pastor.'"

"Excuse me?"

"You say, 'No, Pastor,'" said the old lady in the white cotton dress.

"He already told you that," said a middle-aged man in a gruff, haughty voice. He wore a perfectly pressed Oxford shirt, bright orange suspenders, and creaseless khaki pants. "Why don't you listen, woman?"

Linda was breathing hard, her heart racing and palms damp with sweat. "I... I think I'm gonna go. I'm sorry. But thank you. Thanks... all of you."

She began to rise, and Mary Anne brought a hand down firmly upon her shoulder. "Sit... down." Her smile had vanished completely. Her eyes flashed with choler and a gross determination. "Sit down, *Linda*, and listen to the Pastor."

"I really think -"

"Are you married?" asked the pastor.

"Yes. But -"

"Did you lose your virginity to your husband?"

"Excuse me?"

The pastor now stood and hurled his Bible against the wall. "Did any man *fuck* you before you were married?"

Linda tried to get up again and now several members of the group pinned her to her seat. "I want out of here! Let me go!"

"Have you ever given birth to a bastard child?"

"Let me *go!*" More struggling, all of it futile.

"Have you ever had an abortion?"

Linda was weeping now. "Mary Anne! Please! Tell him why I'm here! Tell him about your car!"

"The car means nothing," said Mary Anne flatly. "Jesus means everything."

"Praise Jesus!" chanted the group. "Praise the Lord, the Son of Man!"

The pastor came to her now, putting his face just inches from hers. "Do you give oral sex to your husband? Do you let him sodomize you? Do you lust after other men? Do you mock our Lord Jesus Christ with your hedonistic lifestyle? *Do* you, bitch?"

Linda writhed in her chair, but three men and Mary Anne held her fast. "I'll call the police! I swear to..." She trailed off, sweat coursing down her face, lank bangs dangling in her eyes.

"Swear to who, Linda? Allah? The Buddha? Some false... fucking... *idol*?" The pastor was screaming now.

"Please! *Please* let me go! I'm only here... I'm only here because..." She broke down crying.

"Because why, Linda? Because you hit our Mary Anne's car with your husband's truck? Because you're too small and stupid and *weak* to control that kind of vehicle?" The pastor spat in her face. "Tell me, Linda, have you ever had a dick in your ass? Have you ever used intravenous drugs? Have you ever masturbated to pornography? Have you ever slept with a *nigger?*"

Linda went on bawling.

"Do you think it's okay... to burn an American *flag?* Do you think the Lord Jesus Christ... *approves...* of a nigger running our country? Do you think schools have the *right...* to take down the Ten Commandments from their hallways? Do you think GOD ALMIGHTY *smiles...* when faggots marry each other? Do you think you'll get into heaven just because you gave a homeless man a dollar, a dollar he used to buy *booze?* Do you think you'll take your diamond ring and your big-screen TV and your marble countertops and king-sized waterbed into heaven with you? Huh? *Do* you?"

Linda couldn't speak. She could only go on sobbing.

"Answer me, bitch!"

"I... I don't know."

"Well it isn't, and He doesn't, and they don't, and He doesn't, and you won't!"

"You won't!" echoed the group.

"Praise Jesus!" cried the young man in the suit and tie.

"Praise Jesus!" repeated the group.

"Mary Anne," said the Pastor, gritting his teeth. A bead of sweat trickled down his brow and the bridge of his nose.

"Yes, Pastor?"

"Aren't we overdue for a sacrifice?"

"I believe we are, Pastor."

"And to whom should we entrust the honor?"

Linda fought again to break free, but it was fruitless. She was trapped.

"I can think of no one better," said Mary Anne, "than Linda's sister-in-law, Ms. Alice Silkowski."

"Brilliant!" yelled the pastor. "Absolutely brilliant!"

Linda thought she was about to faint, hoped *desperately* to faint, but somehow, horribly, remained conscious.

And then she saw Alice emerge from the shadows on the other side of the room. She wore a white hooded robe tied at the waist with a frayed rope. She pulled the hood back slowly, her face cast in the sickening yellow light that emanated from the overhead florescent. She wore the same shade of lipstick as Mary Anne, the same blush, the same eyeliner, the same hairstyle. Her lips curled up in a demented, nauseating smile which made Linda's stomach turn.

"Are you prepared to sacrifice this woman?" Pastor Gibbons asked Linda's sister-in-law.

"I am," replied Alice.

"Bring her forth," instructed the pastor.

The three men and Mary Anne dragged Linda from her chair, Linda kicking and screaming. The faithful members of the Woodford County chapter of the Good Christians' Club all now produced flashlights and shone them on a small wooden altar in the corner of the room, an altar which Linda was sure had not been there when she'd entered.

"Let me go, dammit!" Linda cried. "Let me go or you're all going to prison!"

This induced general laughter among the audience. Mary Anne grabbed her by the hair and tugged on it, making her scream louder. "Move it, bitch!"

Now the members of the group began to sing: "Swing low, sweet chariot, comin' for to carry me home! Swing low, sweet chariot, comin' for to carry me home!"

"Sacrifice!" yelled the pastor. His hair was now as wild as his eyes, falling across his forehead in limp tousles. Linda saw in a muddled flash that his teeth were rotting in his mouth. "It's time for a sacrifice!"

"I looked over Jordan, and what did I see, comin' for to carry me home, a band of angels comin' after me, comin' for to carry me home!"

"I'm *begging* you!" Linda shouted. "I'm *begging* you! Don't do this!"

Alice reached into a deep pocket of her robe and removed a large dagger with a gilded haft. The blade glinted cruelly in the feeble light.

"If you get there before I do, comin' for to carry me home, tell all my friends I'm comin' too, comin' for to carry me home!"

"Lay her down," Alice said. "Lay the whore down."

Mary Anne and her fellow members complied, pinning her to the altar. She wriggled and squirmed, but they held her still enough that Pastor Gibbons could lash her down to the boards made of acacia wood, strapping her wrists and ankles with twine to rivets fixed to the four corners.

The group began to clap and cheer, breaking into another song: "Are you ready for a miracle? As ready as I can be! Are you ready for a miracle? The Spirit will set you free! Are you ready, ready, ready, ready, I'm ready, I'm ready for a miracle!"

"*Stop this!*" yelled Linda.

The pastor leaned over and whispered in her face, his breath hot and sour: "We'll stop nothing, heathen. Wench. *Sinner!*"

"Are you ready for a miracle?" asked the group, still clapping. "As ready as I can be!"

Alice raised the dagger, smiling broadly. Linda closed her eyes, picturing Billy, sitting at home, legs up on the footstool, watching TV, waiting patiently for her return. She pictured her brother and sister, back in Missouri, working on the family farm. She pictured her mother, now dead, and her father, old but steadfast, resolute. She imagined herself as a young girl, jumping rope in the schoolyard, going to birthday parties, kissing a boy for the first time. She wished she had had a child of her own, and still wanted to, but –

"May Jesus Christ accept this sacrifice as thanksgiving for all His mercies and gifts," said the Pastor. "May Jesus Christ bless my righteous congregation at this, the holiest of all times, as the day of the Birth of our Savior draws nigh, and consign this ungodly sinner to the eternal flames of Hades, that untold suffering might be inflicted upon her, forever and ever, Amen."

"Amen," said the group.

"I love your brother with all my heart," Linda said to Alice. Her voice scarcely quavered.

Alice hesitated, glancing over at the pastor and the rest of the congregation.

Pastor Gibbons shook his head solemnly. "Alice, my dear, sinners can't love *anyone*. Not truly. Not in the way Jesus wants them to. Do you understand?"

Alice nodded, raised the dagger again, and closed her eyes.

"He'll never forgive you," Linda said.

"God won't forgive you for shirking your duty," said the pastor.

"Amen!" shouted the group.

Linda sobbed. "I beg you, Alice, not to do this."

Alice looked away for a moment, her eyes briefly meeting the pastor's. He gave her an encouraging nod. She looked back at Linda and said, "I'd rather have God's forgiveness than my brother's."

Somebody had placed a small statue of Jesus at the foot of the altar. Linda looked at it through bleary, tear-filled eyes. Christ's eyes were closed, as if He could not bear to witness the savagery that was about to occur. His hands were clasped together in prayer. Now Linda closed her own eyes and prayed, prayed that there really *was* a heaven, and that she'd go there, and one day see again those whom she desperately loved.

As the dagger pierced her chest, she heard the group begin to pray: "Our Father, who art in Heaven, hallowed be thy Name..."

CAT IN THE MOONLIGHT

I hadn't seen Duncan since he'd lost Missy the winter before. He'd first took leave from the factory, then just quit altogether. I'd tried calling him a dozen times, never got an answer. I half-figured the man for dead.

Until about one o' clock this morning, when he showed up on my doorstep, covered in dried blood. He woke me up with a series of knocks loud enough to rattle the door in the frame. When I finally opened it, he was raving like a loon, jabbering about slitting his finger with a butcher knife. He'd tied a tourniquet around the finger in question. His tan Carharts was streaked and splattered red, his face white as the snow on the ground – except for the meandering trail of blood he'd left in his wake, scarlet beads glinting wanly in the moonlight. And his teeth was chattering. I'll remember that as vividly as anything else, I'm certain of it. I'd never seen a fella's teeth chatter so hard.

"Christ," I said, still half-asleep. I rubbed my eyes, wondering if I was dreaming. "Christ, Duncan, what in good God happened? Get in here, outta the cold."

He sort of half-staggered into my small foyer, then collapsed against a table by the door. "Levi," he said. "I need help."

"Why in Christ's name didn't you call an ambulance? We need to get you to the hospital. That rag ain't gonna hold for long. What -"

"It was all I could find," he said, gesturing vaguely at the oily dust rag he'd wrapped haphazardly around his wounded finger. "I panicked. I don't wanna see no doctor. I just need *help*."

I tried to steady him, told him to put his arm around my shoulder. He did. "Help with what, pal? Where the hell have you been at, anyway? C'mon, follow me into the kitchen."

He followed me on wobbly legs, and I sat him down in one of the chairs at the table. He was shaking all over like a leaf. "I'm losing my mind," he said. He looked like he was about to faint.

"Just calm down," I said, sitting down next to him. I tried to sound calm myself but was getting scared now. I felt an icy sweat break out on my forehead. "Try and take it easy and just tell me what happened."

"I cut myself," he said, as if *that* wasn't obvious. "Cut m'self bad."

"Doin' what? Butcherin' meat?"

He just nodded, then winced in pain and pulled the tourniquet tighter.

"What the hell was you doin' butchering meat at this hour? And why didn't you call for an ambulance? On account of money?"

He nodded again, tears pricking the corners of his eyes. It were evident the man was in serious pain, and I hesitated before asking why he'd chose to come *here*.

"Only... only place I reckoned I could walk to," he said. Mumbled, really.

"Well, will you let me drive you to the hospital? You gotta get some stitches in that finger." I pointed at his hastily bandaged digit. "Look at it," I said. "It's bleedin' clear through that rag. And that rag's filthy, Duncan. You're gonna get an in -"

"I'll manage!" he shouted, startling me so badly I nearly rocked back in my chair. "Now just let it alone and let me talk, dammit! Will ya?"

"Sure," I said, real fear blooming inside me now. "Sure, Duncan. Say whatever it is you need to say."

He'd lowered his head, as if ashamed of his outburst, and now looked up at me. His eyes was wild, on fire. His whole face had changed. It was like he'd put on a mask, a lunatic's mask, while I weren't looking.

"There was a cat on the fence," he said. "A cat perched on a fence, bathing in the moonlight."

I just stared at him blankly. What else could I do?

"It eyes was glowin' green and evil-like. It looked down at me, down at me from the fence it was sittin' on."

Somehow I found my voice again. "What're you talkin' about, Duncan?"

"They was like emeralds, Levi. Like two bright, sinister emeralds just floatin' in the sky. Then it hissed at me."

I wondered now, seriously, if the man weren't mad with fever, if maybe there weren't something more wrong with him than just the gash on his finger. "Is... is that when you cut yourself? When the cat hissed at you?" My voice was a feeble, wavering croak.

Now he gave me the most hideous smile I ever saw. "No," he said, and all of a sudden he weren't shaking no more. All of a sudden he seemed calm as Rupert Lake on a windless day. "That's when I slit her throat."

I was certain I hadn't heard him right, certain my ears was playing tricks on me - and maybe my eyes, too. But still, this awful panic rose up inside me and all I wanted to do just then was to stand up out of that chair and bolt for the back door. But I knew if I tried to make a break for it, he'd be on me like a tiger, slit finger or none. He was bigger and faster than me, and I hardly dared imagine what he'd do to me once he'd caught me.

"Duncan?" I said. It was just a whisper, a thread of a word.

That grotesque smile of his grew wider. "You remember that Kellner woman, don'tcha, Levi?"

"Sure," I said. And I did, vividly. She'd gone missing from town about six months ago, vanished without a trace. She'd been presumed dead since last November. I felt my eyes wanting to dart to the nearest exit, the nearest weapon, but forced them to stay trained on Duncan's. Looking away would mean bad news, I could feel it. "'Course I do."

"She was mine, too."

"Yours?"

He laughed maniacally, tamped down harder on his finger. "Done raped her before I strangled her to death. Had my way with her after, too. I saw the same cat in the moonlight that night, as I remember. Same nasty emerald eyes starin' down at me, like it just come up from hell."

I bit my lower lip, trying to think through the pea-soup fog that had settled down around my brain. I needed a plan, and fast. But first, I figured, I needed to keep him talking. "Up from hell?"

Duncan sneered at me. "You don't think I cut my finger butcherin' that hog, do ya?"

"Well hell," I said, "I'm just tryin' to listen to what you're tellin' me, Duncan. I mean…" I trailed off, a big lump forming in my throat.

He pounded the table with his good fist. "You think I did it to myself. Admit it! I can see it on your face, you sonofabitch!"

"I b-believe you, Duncan. I know how much butcherin' you do. I got no reason -"

"Bitch done it to me," he said. "Finagled the knife outta my hand before I got it back and turned her around and dragged that nice, sharp blade right across her fuckin' throat. Never seen nobody bleed s'damn much. Shit squirted out like water from a hydrant!" He laughed again, more darkly this time.

Then I asked maybe the dumbest question I could have: "What was her name?"

"Don't hardly matter," he said nonchalantly, slowly unwrapping the tourniquet. Incredibly, the bleeding had mostly stopped, was now just seeping out like sludge from a leak in a sewer pipe. "She's cold as the snow outside now."

"Your finger," I said. "The bleeding stopped."

"It stopped a while ago," he replied evenly. "Most of the blood you saw was hers." Now he thumped *both* fists on the table, re-opening his wound a little, and put on a mad grin. "Ha!"

I squirmed in my seat, trying to keep my composure but finding it harder and harder. I didn't want him to see the fear in my eyes. I knew that he could. "Jesus, Duncan. I don't... I don't really know what to say. If you came here to confess, I can promise you your secret's safe with me. I don't rat on friends. But -"

"*Confess?*" he barked, incredulous-like. "You think I came here to *confess?*"

"Well -"

"If I'd come here to confess, I'd be telling you about the other three whores I done killed in other towns. I'd tell you how I drowned one of 'em in a crick, shoved her goddam head down so hard I damned near tore her scalp off when I finally dragged her outta the water by her hair. I'd tell you about the bitch I filleted

115

with a steak knife, just lettin' her guts fall out all over her own kitchen floor." Now he glanced down at *my* kitchen floor. "Weren't all that different from yours, come to think of it. Same color linoleum and everything. Ain't that some shit?"

I just kept on looking at him, for some reason afraid to blink.

He carried on: "And I'd tell you about the pretty little jade I doused with kerosene and then lit on fire. Her screams was like... I dunno, but they went on forever, it seemed like. Maybe it'd be the way a cat sounded if you trapped it in a hot oven. You know, cooked 'er alive." He laughed again, shrill and piercing and wild, his eyes aflame with perverse delight. "Not that I'd ever cook a cat, of course. I like cats, always have. 'Specially when their eyes glow in the moonlight."

I cleared my throat, trying to dislodge (or maybe dissolve) the growing lump. "Well if you didn't come here to confess, Duncan, then what *did* you come here for? If my askin's all right, I mean."

His smiling, dementedly jovial face now turned sour. "You was the most nearby," he said, as if that explained everything. "Thought I said that earlier."

"You said you wanted my help. So what can I do for you?"

He frowned, as though disappointed that I had to ask. "Wantcha to help me dig the hole for her. She's layed up in the freezer in my garage, but that ain't no place to keep her. Got meat to put in there, too. Need the space."

Is this a dream? I wondered again. *Am I dreaming? Surely I must be. Surely this can't really be happening.*

"You want me to help dig the grave," I said distantly, mimicking like a parrot.

"Uh huh. I got this weird feeling from the cat that she wanted me to get you involved in this. It's almost like she *talked* to me, Levi. Ain't that the damndest thing you ever heard?"

"The cat on the fence, you mean."

"Yessir!"

I hesitated, swiped the back of my hand across my mouth. I was still having a hell of a time trying to think clearly. "That *is* something," I said.

Slowly, very slowly, he reached inside his Carharts and drew out a revolver. He placed it gently, almost lovingly on the table. The silver barrel gleamed under the ceiling light. "So what do you reckon, old buddy? Will ya lend a hand?"

"Sure," I said. My heart was thudding at a monstrous pace. I could feel it in my neck and at my temples. "'Course I will, Duncan."

"That's good to hear, Levi. So let's -"

"If you tell me one thing," I said. I regretted it immediately, or at least most of me did, but some other part, brave and defiant, insisted I press on.

He looked at me curiously, mayhap a trace unsettled himself now.

Don't ask it.

But I did: "Did you kill Missy, too?"

His face fell like hot putty oozing down a wall. "You think I'd kill my own *wife*?"

"Now Duncan -"

"You know goddam well she killed herself! Done hung herself, right there in the laundry room! I... I found her dead, Levi. She didn't even bother to leave a note." For the first time since he'd showed up he looked almost sane, and now suddenly burst into tears. Incredibly, part of me actually wanted to comfort the man, to console him, despite the unimaginable things he'd told me, the sundry horrors he'd brought about.

"I'm sorry," I said. I guess, in some weird and ridiculous way, I actually was. "I shouldn't have asked you that."

He just looked away, wiped the tears from his eyes with his good hand. Then he turned back to me, his face stony and clenched, his jaw working. "I got a shovel in my garage. Go get yours." His tone was all business.

My eyes fell to the revolver again. I took a deep breath and stood on legs that felt like circus stilts.

The woman's naked body, already coated in a thick frost, was in the back of Duncan's long-bed Ford pickup, covered by a tarp Duncan had lashed down to the grab rails. Our two shovels was rattling around in the bed.

We drove mostly in silence, except for the occasional meaningless remark by Duncan (at one point he said, "Pyramids hold secrets the way men do, deep in their hearts, but oracles and statues, monuments and cathedrals – they know nothing, mean nothing"). And one comment that made partial sense, and also chilled me to the bone: "When God takes your wife from you, you take God's children from Him. That's the rule." I didn't ask why, if God takes your wife from you, the only children you're supposed to take from Him are women about the same age she was when she died.

I also had no idea where we was going, but was too scared to ask. Somewhere pretty remote, I figured, and when you're already living in the sticks like we was, "pretty remote" means the middle of goddamned nowhere. And where else would you bury a body? In your backyard? I had some odd feeling we was headed for a cemetery, that Duncan actually had a headstone hidden somewhere in the truck and meant to make a proper grave for the woman. But that was absurd, I told myself. No, we wasn't going to no cemetery. We was going into the woods.

His face as he drove was that of a man with great purpose and no purpose at all. It was that stony, rigid face from before, eyes tired but blazing with fervor, teeth gritting and jaw stiff. He kept both hands on the wheel, and I saw his knuckles was swollen and red. I imagined he might've struggled with the woman before he'd managed to subdue her, maybe sprained his hands in the process. I hadn't noticed his hands being like that before, but swelling takes some time, and when a man's bleeding like a stuck pig (or *appears* to be), your eyes tend to see little else.

Eventually we turned down a gravel road that led up a steep hill. There was a yellow sign on the thin strip of shoulder, leaning almost sideways and half-obscured by a tree branch, announcing that the road was a dead end. Another half-mile up there was another sign saying, "WARNING: ROAD NARROWS." That sign weren't lying, neither: by the time we got about two miles into the woods, we was basically riding on a ribbon of snow-covered dirt maybe ten feet wide. I could hear branches scraping against the side panels and windows. For a minute I thought Duncan was going to just keep driving until them trees gobbled us up and we was trapped in the truck. But then he started to slow down, until the truck was barely crawling, and then finally brought it to a stop and cut the engine.

"Get out," he said. It was almost a growl.

I got out. I could hardly open the door for all the tree branches. I had to squirm my way outside, the branches whispering against my big winter coat. A knot on one of them dug into my shoulder and I winced. We both maneuvered our way to the back of the truck and Duncan pressed the latch to release the tailgate.

"Pick up her right leg," he ordered, grabbing her left. "Let's drag this bitch onto the ground."

I took her left foot in my gloved hands and started to pull. She felt like a lead weight, like she was almost glued to the ridges in the bed. Her skin peeled off from it with an awful ripping sound, the sound of velcro coming undone. She landed on the ground with a dull thump.

"Now take her legs and I'll take her arms," Duncan said.

I did as he told me, all the while mindful of the revolver holstered in the back of his waistband. We picked the woman up. Thankfully she was short and skinny, no more than a hundred, maybe a hundred and ten pounds. I saw the frost clinging to the bangs of her flaxen hair and cringed. And when I saw the huge gash across her throat, the blood caked and flaking down to her frozen breasts, my stomach lurched and I thought I might upchuck.

"Quit lollygagging," he said. "We ain't got all night.

"Where we takin' her, Duncan?"

"No questions. Just carry her where I lead you."

Where he led me was deep into a thick stand of oak trees and towering pines growing out of the snow-swept earth and stabbing the night with their jagged crowns. We dropped her body on the ground, same as if we was dropping a block of cement. I felt my stomach turn over again. The way she fell, with her legs splayed and arms laying limp at her sides, she might've been making a snow angel. The thought triggered a whole new revulsion, and a deep sadness, a terrible, guilt-riddled grief that washed over me in a staggering wave.

I guess Duncan saw the disquiet in my features, because he gave me a disapproving look and told me to get my shit together, we had work to do.

And so we did.

It took a good hour, hour and a half to dig a hole maybe three feet deep, four feet wide, and six feet long. By the time we was done I was panting with fatigue. My muscles was taut with exhaustion and strain.

"Help me roll her in," Duncan said. His voice had been calm the whole time, his demeanor icy and detached. Now he sounded utterly sociopathic. I guess he was, always had been, at least since Missy had tied a noose around her neck and let that stool slip out from under her. She'd broke her neck, I'd heard, and when Duncan had sliced through the rope with one of his butcher knives her head had spilt to one side like a rag doll's, a rag doll with half its stuffing yanked out. Any man in Duncan's shoes would've surely lost his mind, just as he had, and despite all the evil things he'd done, a tiny flicker a pity coursed through me. Maybe that's because I'd known him when he was still sane, when sins so wretched as his would've surely been beyond his own comprehension. Or so I told myself.

"I said help me roll her in, Levi."

Shivering from the cold, I squatted and got my hands underneath one of her thighs and gave her a big push. She tumbled into the shallow grave, facedown, and we both let out long, shaky breaths. The only thing left to do now was to refill the hole with the mounds of dirt heaped around it. And that was a good thing, because I thought maybe hypothermia was setting in. Duncan seemed totally unbothered by the cold.

I bent down to retrieve my shovel when I felt something hard and slender press against the back of my head. Of course I knew right off what it was, and I guess part of me had expected it the whole time. I'd tried denying it, tried convincing myself that somehow, if I just did everything he asked without griping or trying to flee, the man would actually trust me to keep my mouth shut and let me live. But deep down I'd known better. Deep down I'd known I was destined to go the same way as the naked woman now lying prostrate in a shallow grave.

"Get in that hole!" Duncan shouted. "Get down in there with that dirty bitch!"

"Please," I begged. "Don't do this. I promised you I'd -"

"I don't give a fuck *what* you promised. Either jump into that goddam hole or I'll put a bullet through your brain and throw you in there myself. Your choice, Levi."

"Okay," I relented, just trying to buy some time. I had no real plan of escape, no exit strategy that immediately leaped to mind. But I hoped and prayed one would come to me if I could just stall long enough. I'd thought about trying to sneak a weapon of some kind into my coat pocket before getting into the truck, but Duncan had watched my every move, never took his eyes off me. So now I was stuck. Now I was a dead man standing, standing and shaking all over just the way he'd been when he'd first showed up at my house.

"Then do it, dammit. Ain't no time to waste."

Slowly, I sat down at the edge of the hole and lowered myself it.

"Now lie down."

For a brief moment I thought about just telling him to shoot me. The thought of being buried alive was unfathomable, maybe more terrifying than any other thought a man could conceive. But still, I clung desperately to life, racking my brain for some way out. Nothing came to me. And so, my heart galloping in my chest, I stretched my legs out and leaned back, on top of the woman's feet. I stand about six-two, so I had to sort of pull my knees up a little just to fit inside the dirt vault. Snow started falling again, flakes hitting my numb red face and melting instantly into freezing-cold rivulets. I thought I might pass out from fear.

Duncan grabbed one of the shovels and started heaping dirt on top of me. Each load hit me like a light brick, sliding off my nylon coat and spattering my pant legs. It sounded like the rattle of the leaves in the wind, like a broom whisking across a dirty floor. I closed my eyes when he started dumping the dirt on my face, swatting it away as best I could in the narrow confines of my makeshift tomb.

"I'm real sorry about this, Levi," he said as he kept shoveling in dirt. "Truly I am." And I'll be damned if the guy didn't sound halfway sincere. "But a fella's gotta do what a fella's gotta do, ya know?"

I just lay there, breathing so heavy I thought I might hyperventilate.

"I asked you a question, Levi."

"I'll pay you," I said, shaking off more dirt. "Every penny I got in the bank."

He laughed and dumped another pile of dirt into the hole. "Hard to spend money when you're locked up. Or riding the lightning up in Moundsville."

"I swear to God I'd never -"

"Already tried that." More dirt. Another heavy thump against my body.

"For Chrissakes!" I bellowed. "We're *friends*, Duncan. We've knowed each other since grade school! How the hell can you *do* this?"

"Got no choice." More dirt. I was almost completely covered now.

"Then why'd you pick me, dammit?" Some soil got into my mouth and I coughed it up. "Just tell me that, I'm beggin' you. Why'd you pick me when you coulda picked anyone? Huh?"

"Done told you," he said, plowing the shovel into a huge mound. "You was closest. And the cat told me to."

"You barely even cut your finger," I protested, spitting more dirt out of my mouth. "You coulda walked to anyone's house you pleased, or drove. And cats don't fuckin' talk, Duncan!"

"This one did. And it don't matter now, anyhow. What's done is done. I guess you just got unlucky."

I steadied my nerves as best I could, my brain whirring with panic. "It's because you found out, ain't it? Because someone told you. Maybe even Missy. Maybe she couldn't stand the guilt."

At that his arms froze in mid-lift. He let the dirt on the shovel just drain down one side of the hole. "What the hell are you talkin' about, Levi? What's Missy got to do with this?"

"You know damn well what she has to do with this," I said. "Or if you don't, then I need to confess it before you finish coverin' me up and I take my last breath. I don't wanna take it with me, Duncan. Please, at least just give me a chance to get it off my chest and clear my conscience so I can die in peace. Can't you at least do *that* for me?"

He threw the shovel to the ground and squatted down next to the hole. "Start makin' sense, or I'll just save myself the work and shoot you where you's lyin'."

"Missy and me," I said, wriggling in the hole. My legs was already going stiff and numb. "We had an affair. For over six months. Mostly when you was at work, sometimes at motels on weekends. I... I was gonna tell you, Duncan, I truly was, but I just couldn't muster the nerve. And then Missy... well, after she did what she did, I couldn't bear the thought of puttin' that kinda hurt on you, causin' you more heartache than you already had."

His eyes got big as silver dollars. His cheeks, already red, now turned a deep, burning crimson. His hands was quivering, his legs turning to jelly. The man was ten shades of irate. "You fucked my *wife*?" he screamed. "And that's why she killed herself? Is that what you're tellin' me, you worthless sack-a shit?"

"I'm so sorry, Duncan. I'm… I just don't know what I was thinkin'."

"You lyin' to me, motherfucker?"

"I wish I was."

He just stared at me for a minute, a minute that seemed to stretch on for eternity. I knew in that moment my life was within seconds of reaching its end. He reached around to his back waistband and unleashed the revolver. He could barely hold it steady.

"Duncan, please." I was sobbing now.

"You don't even deserve…" He was panting heavy, the revolver bobbing up and down in his hand. He could hardly aim it at me. "You don't even *deserve* a goddam burial, you sonofabitch! Traitor! Cheater!"

"Duncan, I -"

"*Bastard!*" he screamed. Tears was coursing down his cheeks. "I… you…" His panting got heavier. "I'm gonna fuckin'…" And then he shot the pistol, missing my head by about an inch. The report was deafening, echoing in the woods like the howl of a ghost. Dirt flew up and sprinkled my face.

And then, abruptly, he started keeling backward. He collapsed to his knees. "Oh, Christ," he muttered. I could barely hear him, but I thought I knew what was happening.

He clutched his chest, let out a terrific groan of pain, started wheezing.

"Duncan?" I said. "Are you all right?"

"My... my heart," he grunted.

I sat up, meaning to pull myself out of the hole.

"No," he said, and took another blind, wild shot. This one just vanished in the wind.

"Duncan, let me -"

And then he collapsed completely, lying facedown on the ground, just like the dead woman underneath me. He let out a faint, choked breath and then fell silent. He lay there on the forest floor, perfectly still, and there was no sound save the hoot of an owl and that soft rustling of leaves in the wind.

I was horribly indecisive about what to do once I'd climbed out of what had almost become my final resting place. My first thought was to just roll Duncan's body into the hole and bury him along with his victim, let him turn up missing and, if his body was ever found, either hope the cops never linked it back to me or, if they did, just tell them the truth. But then I realized how stupid that was, how risky. What reason would the police have to believe me, other than my reputation around town and lack of a criminal record? Should I just leave his body where it was, then, and call the police when I got home? But even then they might think *I* killed the woman.

On the other hand, why the hell would a sane, decent person tell the police such a story if he *was* the real killer? How could the real killer even *be* sane, much less decent? I was in a hell of a bind and I knew it. None of my choices was all that appealing, and none seemed all that safe, either.

So I got the keys out of Duncan's coat pocket and got in the truck and cranked the heat so I could think more clearly. In the end, after about five minutes of debating it, I decided I'm simply drive home, call the cops, and tell them the truth. After wiping my prints off my shovel, of course. And making sure his stayed on his own.

I looked over at Duncan's body (*corpse,* I thought, *it's a goddamned* corpse) and felt a chill run up my spine. He was a monster, a moral monster, and he'd deserved to die for what he done. It was *him* who didn't deserve a proper burial, or even cremation, which he'd probably get after the coroner did the autopsy. What he deserved was to be buried in a hole even cruder and shallower than the one we'd dug for the poor woman he'd murdered. And I reflected, too, how close I'd come to death, how only an act of God had saved me.

I shivered and started the truck, drove it back to Duncan's trailer. My hands was still trembling when I got there.

I started the short walk back to my own place, wrapping my arms around myself in a mostly fruitless effort to warm myself up. I could see my breath on the air, puffing out in wispy clouds like cigarette smoke. It was close to dawn by then, and a total exhaustion had set in, body and mind alike. My feet felt like cement blocks. All I wanted to do was to make that dreadful phone call, get it over with, and go straight to bed. And yet sleep seemed impossible. I was a live wire, terrified somebody would drive along and spot me carrying a shovel.

But nobody did. And when my house came into view, finally, I let out a heavy sigh of relief. I was almost there, almost safe.

And then I saw them: crazed green eyes ablaze in the moonlight, perfectly round with dilated pupils somehow darker than the early morning sky. They were awful things, ominous and hypnotic, glaring at me with an intensity that froze me where I stood. They were haunting.

All at once I felt my feet begin to move again, as if of their own will, as if drawn forward by those baleful eyes which never blinked. Soon enough I was but mere feet from my front porch. The cat was sitting on the top step, still and purposeful, its long black tail curled around its body, its fur mangy and slick, like somebody'd bathed it in oil. Its eyes never left mine.

Somehow, after a long moment, I was able to look away. I glanced down at my shovel, saw I was gripping the handle so tight my knuckles was white as lilies.

Kill it, I thought. *You have to kill it before it infects you, before it turns your heart into stone.*

I took the handle in both hands now, began to raise the blade, meaning to swing at the cat's head with the underside, to crush its skull and blind those treacherous eyes forever.

But when I looked up again it was gone. It had scurried off into the night, and though I looked in all directions, I could see it nowhere. It was as if it had never been there in the first place.

Maybe it wasn't.

Shuddering, I fished my house key out of my coat pocket and opened the door fast, closing it just as quick behind me. I locked it and slid the deadbolt into place. Then I just stood there for a minute, shaking and letting the warmth of the house wash over me. I let out a long, hitching breath. I remembered the shovel in my hand and leaned it against the table by the door.

I went into the kitchen and looked at the phone on the wall. I looked at it for a long time. But all I could really see was them foreboding green eyes, gleaming madly in the dark, hungry and unblinking.

I turned and went back through the kitchen to the foyer and plodded up the stairs. I undressed slowly and got into bed.

I didn't sleep till well past daybreak, and my slumber was shallow, saturated with ghastly nightmares the likes of which I'd never dreamt before. I woke up gasping for air, just after twilight, just as the sky was beginning to darken again.

I got up and looked out my window at the pale moonlight, dreading what I might see perched atop the fence in my backyard. But there was only a sparrow, which took flight a moment later. And then there was nothing.

I dressed and went downstairs, into the foyer. At first I almost didn't notice it, but then caught it out the corner of my eye.

Black fur clung to the blade of the shovel like flies on rotting meat.

THE FORTUITOUS DEATH OF
DR. ALFRED W. PRESTON

I. A LONG SICKNESS

His name was Alfred Wilson Preston. He held doctorate degrees in Philosophy and Logic, both from Harvard. He and his young wife made their home in a rural town in Connecticut, attracted to the relative seclusion. Occasionally Dr. Preston would serve as a guest lecturer at Yale, but he spent most of his time writing and publishing books and articles. He drew a modest income from them, but scarcely needed it: he had, upon his father's death, inherited a veritable fortune, a sum well exceeding a million dollars. He and his wife owned a sprawling manor, kept a half-dozen full-time servants, but otherwise lived simply, giving most of their wealth to various charities.

Alfred's wife's name was Julia. He was forty-two, she twenty-seven. She was a musician and a painter, a wonderful painter, selling many of her works to prominent collectors. She had her own studio on the grounds, in which she spent whole days while Alfred plugged away at this treatise or that. They had married in the spring of 1876, but had yet, ten years later, to produce issue. They had both long suspected that either she was infertile or he sterile, but had never stopped trying, all the same. They both desperately wanted a child.

Julia's health had been on the decline lately, and it worried Alfred terribly. Why should such a robust young woman fall so violently ill so often? There were bouts of awful vertigo and nausea, attended often by nasty regurgitations. She complained frequently of bad headaches and drowsiness, suffered periodic confusion. She had grown steadily paler and weaker, spending now as much time in bed as she did in her studio. But still, she had refused to see a doctor, convinced the spells would pass. Alfred was less sure.

Presently he was working, as best he could in his distracted state, on a putative solution of the Liar's Paradox. He had been tempted simply to reject self-referential statements as meaningless, but now thought there might be a way to actually prove the Liar's statement strictly *false*. The prospect of this excited him terribly – or would have, were he not so worried about Julia.

He had just picked up his pen when he put it down again. He glanced at his desk, at the bottomless reams of notes scattered about its surface, most of them bearing what Julia called his "mad genius chicken-scratch." And it would have been, indeed, largely indecipherable to most anyone but him, not only in its illegibility but in its murky content as well. He wrote in a kind of private shorthand, quite frenziedly when inspiration struck him. Now all of it seemed meaningless to him, too. Now his mind was focused entirely on his wife.

He sighed, pushed aside the sheet paper on which he'd been scribbling logical notation, and rose from his desk. It was tea time, and whereas Julia had once prepared supper diligently every evening (both she and her husband thought the servants' time better spent on housework), of late the task had fallen upon Alfred. It was not a taxing chore, however, as Julia was an exceptionally picky eater who habitually craved bread and soup. She had had it for dinner, almost invariably, for the past three months. Alfred was convinced her constancy of diet lent heavily to her recent ailing, that her blood was deficient in protein and sundry other important nutrients, but she would hear none of it. Every night she clamored for her blasted bread and soup, and Alfred served it dutifully.

He started now for the kitchen, passing Claudia in the hallway. She wore a white bonnet and powder-blue apron, carried in her arms a big wicker basket full of laundry. "Sir," she said, favoring him with a nod.

"Claudia."

She started on her way again, then paused. "Sir?"

"Yes, Claudia?"

She frowned sincerely but deferentially. "How's the Missus, sir?"

"She's all right, Claudia." A grandfather clock chimed in the parlor. "It's tea time. Have you seen her?"

"I believe she's in bed, sir."

"Ah. Would you wake her in ten minutes? Or have Beatrice do it?"

Claudia nodded obediently. "Yes, sir. I thought perhaps I could be of some assistance in the kitchen this evening?"

Alfred shook his head, smiling appreciatively. "No, Claudia, that's quite all right. But thank you for the kind offer."

"Of course, sir." She nodded again, gave a wan little smile, and continued through the hall.

Alfred turned and carried on to the kitchen.

*   *   *

"You really must eat more," Alfred advised his wife solemnly, placing the bowl and plate carefully on her bed tray. "This diet is making you ill."

"It's just a bad spell," she countered firmly. She sat up in the bed, taking the spoon in her hand. Her skin was waxy, pallid, her eyes dull and listless. "If it hasn't passed by month's end, I'll see Dr. Verlane." She eyed him curiously. "Satisfied?"

He sighed, far from satisfied. "I suppose."

She glanced into the bowl. "Beef and vegetable tonight?"

"You need the nutrition."

"You know I prefer a simpler soup, Alfred. Tomato, for instance, or mushroom. Or pea."

"You need protein," he said.

"I think meat makes me ill."

"Nonsense."

"I might be allergic to it. The same way you're allergic to flour."

"Then confirm it with Dr. Verlane!" He'd raised his voice without meaning to, and her hand now froze in mid-air. The spoon trembled a bit between her fingers, spilling a few drips of soup back into the bowl.

He took a breath and put his hand to his forehead. "I'm sorry," he said. "I didn't mean to shout."

She plunked the spoon into the bowl and averted her eyes. "I believe I'll eat my bread first tonight." She lifted the slice of wheat to her mouth and noshed on the crust.

"Whatever you wish, dear. I'll be back in a few minutes to check on you."

He went toward the door, and she called after him: "Solved the Paradox yet, my love?"

"Still tackling it," he said without turning around.

Though their servants usually purchased the household groceries, once in a while Alfred himself took a notion to do so, enjoying as he did the occasional outing. The Preston estate was located on the eastern border of Timford, about three miles from the town's sole grocer. It was a twenty-minute trip by horseback.

Alfred set out today, a cold, snowy day, on Samantha, a placid black mare with a gorgeous mane. He had left instructions for Claudia and Marie to keep a close eye on Julia. She'd had another episode that morning, a terrible fit of vomiting that had left her bedridden and dehydrated. The two servants were to monitor her vigilantly, supplying water and whatever meager fare she felt able to stomach. They seemed as concerned about her condition as he, and Alfred supposed that was only to be expected: they were the longest-serving help, having come aboard the year after he and Julia had married.

As he rode the snow pelted his face, and he pulled his wool cap tighter around his head. Samantha whinnied, as if protesting the cold, but pressed on obediently. They rode over knolls and hills, across a frozen brook, between stands of bare trees and around a shallow bog rendered now a bowl of crusted ice. Heavy clouds glided piecemeal through a gray sky, foretelling an evening blizzard.

Soon he arrived in town. He hitched Samantha at the post outside the general store and made his way inside, into the relative warmth. A three-log fire crackled pleasantly in a wood stove in one of the corners. Samuel Caldwell, both Timford's town sheriff and the Sheriff of Sanford County, stood at the counter, making idle chitchat with old Herman Gibbs, the shop's keeper since time immemorial.

"Dr. Preston," Herman said, raising a hand.

"Herman."

"Ain't seen you 'round these parts in a while."

"Nor I," added the Sheriff.

Alfred smiled, removing his cap. "When I come, I stock up."

"Only way to do it in the wintertime," said Herman.

"How's that pretty wife of yours?" Caldwell asked.

"Not so well," Alfred said. He stepped up to the counter, pointing to a bag of flour and a box of dates. "I'll take those."

Herman retrieved the dates, hesitated for a moment, and then selected a bag of flour from the far right of the shelf. He set them on the counter, started scribbling in his ledger with the stub of a pencil. "Still having them dizzy spells, is she?"

"I'm afraid so. Terrible nausea, as well."

"Careful with that flour," Caldwell said. He knew Alfred was allergic to the stuff.

"I'll put another sack around it," Herman said. "What else can I get for you, Doctor?"

"A jar of currants, three quarts of milk, four sticks of butter, a box of salt, and six cans of soup."

"Which soups?"

"Four tomato, one pea, one beef and vegetable."

Herman gathered the items in question, set them on the counter, and then jotted them down in his ledger and drafted a receipt for Alfred. The Sheriff simply watched, picking his teeth with a toothpick. "I sure hope she gets better," he said around the pick.

"I'm sure she will." Alfred smiled again and collected his things, placing them carefully into his two satchels.

"How's the professing business?" Caldwell asked him, a little grin rising at the corners of his lips. For some reason, Alfred rather didn't care much for it.

"Just lovely," he said. "How's the law enforcement business?"

Caldwell appeared to consider for a moment. "More interesting than the architecture business ever was," he said, and his grin became more prominent.

"Quite a load to haul there," Herman observed, sliding the receipt across the counter. Alfred picked it up and slipped it into his coat pocket.

"I'll manage."

Herman nodded and smiled, straightening his apron. His spectacles sat precariously on the edge of his nose, under beady brown eyes and bushy white eyebrows. Exactly three white hairs sprang up in curls from his otherwise perfectly bald, round, liver-spotted head. "See you next time, Dr. Preston."

"See you then."

The ride home was long and grueling, Samantha voicing ample discontent at the weight of the satchels. By the time they arrived home, he was chilled to the bone, and Julia fast asleep.

Weeks passed. Julia seemed to rally briefly before her condition rapidly deteriorated. She began to complain of difficulty seeing in dim light and noticed trace amounts of blood in her urine. One night she vomited so much she nearly fainted. Alfred held her as she leaned over a waste bin, holding her under her arms, stroking her hair. She complained of dizziness, pain in her abdomen, and a burning sensation in her throat. Claudia brought a jug of water and Beatrice a cold wash towel.

"Darling?" said Alfred. "Can you stand?"

"No," Julia said weakly.

"Do you need to throw up again?"

"I... I don't know."

Beatrice applied the washcloth. Julia groaned. Claudia shot Alfred a nervous look. "Send for Dr. Verlane," he said. "Tell Thomas to take Samantha, and to tell Verlane that it's urgent."

"No!" cried Julia.

"Hush, woman! I'll hear none of it."

"But Alfred -"

"You'll see the doctor and that's final."

Dr. Verlane arrived within the hour.

"I'm afraid she isn't well," Dr. Verlane said grimly, having briefly examined her. She was now only semi-conscious. "Not well at all."

"How bad is it?"

Dr. Verlane gestured toward the door. "Let's step into the hallway, shall we?"

Alfred followed the doctor into the hallway, closed the door behind him. His heart had sped up a bit, a light sweat breaking out on his palms. "Tell me, doctor: is it bad?"

Dr. Verlane drew in a deep breath, let it out, and put a hand on Alfred's shoulder. "She won't make it, I'm afraid."

Alfred reeled. The hallway shrank, expanded, shrank again. Everything went gray, and for a moment he thought he might faint himself.

"Steady there, Dr. Preston."

"She won't *make* it?"

Dr. Verlane shook his head. "I don't think so. She's... she's been *poisoned*, sir."

"Poisoned? With what?"

"Arsenic, I would suspect."

"How on earth can you tell *that*?"

Dr. Verlane set his bag down. "From her symptoms, of course. Her pallor, weakness, the swelling of her face, her fainting spells, constriction of her throat. Her severe diarrhea, the presence of blood in her vomit and stool. And particularly the white bands across her fingernails, hair loss, and the white fur on her tongue. It isn't the flu, Dr. Preston. It isn't a stomach bug. It's come on gradually, over the course of months. Were it cholera or dysentery, she'd be dead by now. It's no disease or malady *within* her, Dr. Preston. It's from without. It's of sinister import. Poisoning is the best explanation. And given the longevity of her illness, increasingly large quantities of arsenic, over time, is the most plausible candidate."

Alfred ran a hand down his cheek. "But... that's impossible. I monitor her food intake. I inspect everything she eats. I prepare it myself. I..." He paused, looked more closely at Dr. Verlane. There was something in his eyes, something dark and distrustful. "Dr. Verlane, you don't... you don't think *I* had anything to do with this, do you?" His eyes widened, aflame with ire and incredulity. "Do you?"

Dr. Verlane bit his lower lip. "Dr. Preston... Alfred... I make no accusations."

"The devil you don't! I see it in your eyes! You think me a murderer, don't you? Why, this is preposterous!"

"Dr. Preston, try to calm down. I -"

"Calm down? Calm down? How on *earth* am I supposed to *calm down*? You've come to my home to treat my wife, told me she's going to die, all but pronounced me the perpetrator of her impending demise, and you expect me to be *calm*?"

Claudia now poked her head out the door. "Everything all right, sir?"

"It's fine, Claudia. Just stay with Julia, please."

"Yes, sir."

Claudia closed the door, and Alfred turned back to the doctor. "I think you should go now," he said.

"I understand."

"I won't accept what you've said."

"It's your right."

"Begone!"

Alfred instructed Thomas, his butler, to show the doctor out. "And lock the door behind him," Alfred said.

He went back into the bedroom, where Claudia sat beside the bed with her hands clasped around one of Julia's and Beatrice went on dabbing Julia's forehead with the washcloth. "How is she?" he asked. She appeared to be sleeping.

"Out," said Beatrice. "But comfortable, I think."

"Mind her while I go down to the kitchen for a minute, won't you?"

The two ladies nodded. Alfred left the room, took the stairs, and entered the sprawling white kitchen, complete with bay window and sky-light. He went directly to one of the cupboards, opened it, and removed the bag of flour he'd purchased that afternoon. He carried it over to the big island countertop and set it down and opened a drawer, from which he fished a box of stove matches. Turning the bag over, he lit a match and held it close to the small print stamped near the bottom: "THIS FLOUR BAGGED RIGHT HERE AT HERMAN'S GENERAL STORE!"

Alfred blew the match out and tossed the stick into the wastebasket.

Poisoned, he thought. It was a slippery, incorrigible thought, shifting from side to side as he tried to think it squarely. *Arsenic. Slowly. Over time.*

He looked back at the bag, the print now obscured by darkness, and then, on a whim, dumped the remainder of the flour into the trash, along with the burlap sack itself. He washed his hands thoroughly in the basin and dried them on a towel, and then, on ponderous legs, trudged back upstairs.

He rather knew what he would find before he even opened the door. Perhaps it was prescience, or perhaps it was just a well-educated guess of the sort he was paid handsomely to make. In either event, he was right: inside the room, his two servants stood over the bed, Beatrice weeping openly, Claudia's face buried in her hands.

"Is she...?"

Beatrice nodded mournfully, her eyes awash with pity and grief. Alfred collapsed where he stood.

II. A BRIEF DETENTION

It was on the day before the funeral that, rather early in the evening, a heavy knock came upon the main entrance to the manor, startling Alfred from a bleak reverie. He had been reading in the library, but his mind had kept wandering, kept conjuring up dour images of Julia's casket and the damp soil in which soon it would lie.

Now he sat slowly upright, the book sliding off his lap and onto the settee, wondering if perhaps his ears weren't playing tricks on him. Then, refuting the notion soundly, another knock came, this one louder and brisker. Alfred rose, supposing Thomas had already retired for the evening, and made his way into the foyer. "Who is it?" he called.

A gruff voice came back through the door: "Sheriff Caldwell, Dr. Preston. Please let me in. I need to speak with you about a rather urgent matter." There was a sudden clap of thunder, followed by a brilliant bolt of lightning which lit up the entire foyer. Rain drummed against the roof with a steady patter.

Alfred swallowed thickly. "What... matter might that be, Sheriff?"

"Please," Caldwell repeated. "Open the door, Dr. Preston. This manner of subject is best discussed face-to-face."

Now Thomas emerged from his chambers, looking ruffled and sleepy. "I apologize, Master Preston," he said groggily. "I simply lay down for a moment, and the next thing I knew..."

"I have a warrant," the Sheriff said now.

Thomas froze where he stood, alarm driving slumber from his features with a ferocious celerity. "Sir? What's the matter?"

"What sort of warrant?" Alfred asked timidly.

"Open the blasted door, Dr. Preston!"

Now, finally, Alfred went to the door and unlatched the lock, swinging the door inward. "Is this about Julia?"

Raindrops pinged against Sheriff Caldwell's navy blue helmet, coursing down its brim in silvery rivulets. His black slicker cast back flickers of candlelight from inside the foyer in dim, watery strobes, his gold badge glinting dully. "Dr. Alfred W. Preston," the Sheriff intoned, producing a pair of iron handcuffs, "you are hereby under arrest for the murder of your wife."

"You poisoned her," the Sheriff said matter-of-factly, as if hoping to elicit an immediate confession. They sat in a small interrogation room at the Timford station house, Caldwell on one side of a table and Alfred on the other. "The Reinsch test performed by the toxicologist confirmed the presence of a heavy metal in her bloodstream, and the Marsh test confirmed that metal to be arsenic. And the coroner noted significant inflammation and ulceration of her stomach lining."

Alfred stared at Caldwell in utter disbelief. "What possible motive would I have for murdering my wife, Sheriff?"

"Your motive is quite irrelevant, Dr. Preston. Perhaps she'd cuckolded you, or you'd taken a lover of your own and concluded that dispatching your wife was simpler and far cheaper than divorce. Or maybe she'd simply become an intolerable nag, constantly interfering with your work. The point is, it scarcely matters. What *matters*, Dr. Preston, is the *proof*, the physical evidence, that she was murdered. And as you yourself admitted to Dr. Verlane on the night of her death, it was *you* who prepared her meals, supervised her food intake. Not your maids, not your servants."

Alfred yanked at the cuff chaining him to the table, chafing his wrist. It made his skin burn. "I wasn't cuckolded! And I was never unfaithful to Julia! There was no strife between us. I loved her dearly. I've been utterly distraught since her passing, as any of my help will tell you. This... this is simply *ludicrous*." Tears had begun to well up in his eyes.

"It isn't difficult to feign grief, Dr. Preston. Nor is it particularly difficult to conceal adultery. The findings of the inquest, coupled with Dr. Verlane's observations of your wife's condition on the night of her death, are more than sufficient to charge you with homicide, sir. And in light of what you told Dr. Verlane, there's little doubt that the medical experts' testimony at trial will be *amply* sufficient to convict you." Now the Sheriff leaned in closer, regarding Alfred sternly, resolutely, almost (Alfred would have sworn) triumphantly. "But if you'll simply plead guilty to the crime, Doctor, I'm sure the District Attorney would recommend a far more lenient sentence than you if wasted the taxpayers' hard-earned money on a pointless trial. And a conviction of first-degree murder would mean life behind bars in the state penitentiary. Or, worse yet, the old noose.

"On the other hand, if you just make it easy on yourself and confess, I reckon old Mr. Greeley might push for a maximum of twenty, maybe even just fifteen years in a less restrictive facility. A long stretch, to be sure, but a hell of a lot less than thirty or forty. And far less daunting, surely, than the gallows."

Alfred's hands had begun to tremble, beads of perspiration rising on his brow. "Verlane's a quack!" he blurted through a sob, as if that should dispose of the matter entirely.

Caldwell smiled, lifted his legs and rested his snakeskin boots on the table. He crossed one ankle over the other, rubbing a finger along his bottom lip. "He's *your* physician, Dr. Preston. *You* summoned him to your home the night that your wife died, did you not? He's standing outside to corroborate all this, should you disagree."

"How was I to know he'd make such a diagnosis upon evidence so meager, much less that he would endeavor to implicate *me*? I was under severe emotional duress. I should've -"

"You sent for him," the Sheriff said, shrugging. He brought his legs down. "Plain and simple. And he reported his observations to me the very next morning. The inquest was conducted yesterday, confirming his suspicions. It all adds up, sir. And it all points directly to *you* as the culprit."

Alfred glared at him, tears streaming down his flushed cheeks. "Nonsense. I want a lawyer."

"You want a lawyer, do you? Fair enough. But first we've got to book you. And then incarcerate you."

"*Incarcerate* me? I'll post bail!"

"Bail?" Caldwell chuckled derisively. "For a capital crime? Not a chance, Alfred. No, you'll be in jail until you stand trial. That is, if you're foolish enough to *go* to trial."

And that was the end of the interrogation.

He was there that day, Alfred thought now, as he was led out in handcuffs and leg irons. *Caldwell was there, at the store. Smiling just as pretty as you please. He even asked about Julia, and reminded me to be careful not to touch the flour. He's known Gibbs for donkey's years.*

"Keep your legs moving." Caldwell poked him in the back with a baton.

Maybe he and Herman were in on it together. But why? What would either stand to gain from framing me?

"We're nearly there now."

And Herman always took the bags of flour from the far right of the shelf, didn't he? Every time, as if he were being careful to select the right one.

"What will happen to my home?" Alfred asked. A bulb had gone off in his head.

"County will take it, I reckon, along with all your assets. The estate will be put up for auction at a public sale. That's what happens when there's no direct heir and the deed-holder is arrested for a capital crime."

"No direct heir?"

"Spouse or child," Caldwell said impatiently, and prodded him in the back again with his baton. "Just keep walking."

"And what happens if I'm acquitted?"

"Then your assets will be returned to you, the buyer of your estate will be reimbursed for his expenditure, and the deed will be placed back in your name." He paused for a moment, a subtle and perverse grin taking form on his countenance. "But none of that's going to happen, Dr. Preston, because you're *not* going to be acquitted."

"I'm innocent, goddam you!"

Sheriff Caldwell ignored Alfred's protest, strapped a Springfield rifle over his shoulder, and mounted his horse, preparing to lead the procession. Two deputies waited with side arms and batons beside another pair of horses. "You'll be riding on the saddle pad behind Joseph," said one of the deputies. "I'll be following."

Alfred thought of Samantha, of her being locked up in her stable, hungry and cold. He wished badly that she were here, that he might mount her and ride off on her, get away from all this madness. He would ride toward the sunset, through snow or rain, and go

---

wherever she took him. He would be glad to wind up anywhere just now.

"Get on her," Joseph said, unfastening Alfred's shackles. Alfred did so. The deputy mounted in front, settling into the saddle. He grabbed the reins, squeezed the horse's sides with his legs. The horse whinnied and got moving.

They started off toward the jailhouse in Gunphrey, the county seat, heading away from the sun. The deputy kept the reins loose, whipping the mare when the Sheriff yelled that they needed to move faster. Another storm might be moving in, he said, and with the temperature now well below freezing point, such a storm would likely take the form of another blizzard.

"Giddyup!" yelled the deputy. The mare moved faster, joggling Alfred up and down, from side to side. His hands were still cuffed behind his back and maintaining his balance, especially in crossing gusts, was extremely difficult. The cold wind nipped at their faces, ruffled their hair and clothes. About five minutes into the journey, all the horses suddenly stopped.

"What's going on?" hollered the deputy escorting Alfred.

"Somethin's spooked 'em," the Sheriff called back.

"What is it?"

And then it emerged from a stand of bushes alongside the trail: a Canadian water viper, a manner of beast scarcely seen on land. Canadians were one of three species of snakes in New England that were occasionally seen in the wintertime, and only one of two poisonous breeds, the other being the timber rattlesnake (even more seldom spotted this time of year). During the cold seasons they typically lived in the depths of lakes and rivers, where the water was warmest, coming ashore only for easy prey. They were huge, rust-colored serpents with vermilion bands, traditionally dining on large fish and small mammals. They were notoriously aggressive. For one to come ashore in such harsh conditions meant it was either sick or starving or both, in which case it was likely to be even *more* rapacious.

"We've got a Canadian here!" Joseph shrieked.

"A Canadian?" yelled back the other deputy.

"Just keep still," said the Sheriff, turning his horse around. "Keep still and don't say another word."

The deputies complied. Meanwhile, Alfred had no intention of passing up such a golden opportunity. He wasn't likely to encounter another. So he leapt, face-first, onto the hard damp ground, scrambling to his feet before the deputies had even registered what he'd done. Once he was upright, their eyes turned from the snake to him, wide-eyed and disbelieving.

"Hey!" one of them yelled. "Hey, Sheriff, our man's trying -"

"Didn't I tell you to be *quiet*?" the Sheriff called back.

"But he's escaped!"

"Who? Preston?" The Sheriff now saw Alfred scurrying through the bushes and into an open field. "Aim for his arms or legs, dammit! I want him alive! Do you understand me? *I want that man taken alive!*"

The Sheriff and his two deputies raised their side arms and aimed for the shambling fugitive, taking potshots which missed by several feet. And then, eventually, the Sheriff himself struck Alfred in his right shoulder. Alfred howled in pain, fell to one knee, and then forced himself to get up, to keep moving. He ran as fast as his legs would carry him, blood gushing from the bullet wound. Sheriff Caldwell ordered his boys to follow him on their horses, but the Canadian viper was still slithering about and the horses would take no heed.

"For Christ's sake!" Alfred heard Caldwell cry distantly.

"Should we run after him?" one of the deputies asked.

"Hold on," said Caldwell. He raised his rifle, pointed it directly at the snake, and fired. The serpent's skull exploded, the rest of its body writhing wildly in the weeds. Soon it fell still, a mutilated carcass on the side of the trail. But the horses were now doubly spooked, horrified by the gunshots. And Alfred was no longer in sight.

"Let the horses settle," Caldwell said. "We'll find him soon enough. He won't make it far on foot, not in this weather. But when we find him, I want him brought in alive. He won't be taking the easy way out. Not on *my* watch."

So they dismounted, and waited. The sun was beginning to set. Eventually the horses calmed down. The Sheriff and his boys remounted, grabbed the reins, and rode into the field, tracking the trail of their man, Dr. Alfred W. Preston.

III. AN UNFORTUNATE TURN OF EVENTS

Alfred scurried down a slope, and then trudged up another. He hobbled through a small grove of trees and slid down a frost-laden hill. His right shoulder slumped, bleeding profusely, a wellspring of excruciating pain. Only because of the vast rush of adrenaline coursing through his body was he able, just barely, to ignore it.

There lay before him now a great round field of ice surrounded by tall, dead grass and sloping elms. He had no idea where he was going, just knew that he had to get as far from the trail as he could. He needed time to think, to figure out who had killed his wife and how best to bring him to justice. Already the wheels in his head were turning; already suspicions were forming.

He was there that day, he thought again. *Caldwell was there with Herman, at the store. They were talking, laughing. Something about Caldwell's manner seemed unusual. It seemed... well, almost lighthearted. Rather too lighthearted, given the gravity of my wife's condition.*

But why would Sheriff Caldwell want to see Julia dead? What could he gain from it? It made no sense. Unless –

Alfred stopped cold, sitting down on a big rock. A thought had flashed through his mind, hazy and inchoate, dissolving before he could grasp it firmly. Frustrated, he lifted himself up on his thighs and wrestled with the handcuffs for a moment, tried breaking the chain against the rock. But it was no use, the effort leaving him faint and breathless. He plunked back down on the rock and looked over his shoulder. There was no sign, as yet, of the Sheriff or his deputies. But there would be soon.

He let his head droop for a moment, still trying to catch his breath, and then looked up at the frozen lake that stretched out before him, a raven perched on its far bank. A strong gust rippled the few remaining leaves on the trees, causing the bird to take flight. And then, suddenly, it all came together.

If I were dead, Alfred thought, *then, as per my will, with Julia gone, my nephew would inherit my estate. But if I'm incarcerated, then, according to state law, the county takes it, provided mine is the sole interest in the property, which it is. So with Julia dead, and me in jail, all of my property would belong to the county. It would be set for auction, the terms of which to established by the County Commissioner, no doubt with substantial input from Caldwell. Such terms could be subtly rigged. Bids could be deemed ineligible or disqualified for any number of reasons, legitimate or discreetly manufactured. Bids could be improperly submitted or erroneously recorded. And who do you suppose will ensure that Gibbs's is the highest bid of all those officially accepted by the County Clerk's office?*

He still remembered his lawyer advising him of such facts when he closed on the estate. Covering all contingencies, the fellow had called it. And Alfred remembered it, because he remembered everything. He even –

That was when he felt the white-hot pain, six small knives stabbing his lower left calf. He leapt and shrieked. He looked down and saw a Canadian water viper a few feet away, hissing fiercely with its head reared. This one was slightly smaller than the last, its tail shorter and thinner. There were tatters of flesh stuck to its pink fangs. Flesh, fabric, and hair.

How could there be another such snake on land in this weather? Is it sick as well? Starving? Or is it simply a female the male was hunting as a mate?

Alfred rolled up his pant leg and looked down at his calf, beheld an awful sight. He gasped, coughed. A wave of dizziness struck him hard and sent him reeling backward, nearly toppling him. He steadied himself against a tree and looked back at the bite mark, four round gashes above two slightly smaller lacerations. Already his leg had begun to swell, and it felt now as if a small fire had been ignited within it.

His pulse racing, he careened around the bank of the lake and lurched into another stand of woods, this one far larger. This one was a veritable forest. He stumbled around its trees and shrubs like a pinball, endeavoring fruitlessly to calm himself and summon to mind some remedy, however slapdash and temporary, for a venomous snakebite. He knew it was ill-advised to cut into the wound and attempt to extract the poison by mouth, despite popular folk wisdom, and he had no tool with which to make an incision, anyhow. He could use his belt as a tourniquet to prevent or slow the venom from spreading through his bloodstream, but being handcuffed, he had no way even to *remove* his belt, much less lash it around his upper calf.

His mind was growing foggier by the minute, his panic burgeoning despite his best efforts to quell it. His heart rate was rapidly increasing. He knew he needed to be still, to rest, but he would rather die than be detained once more by Caldwell and his deputies. So he kept moving, kept slogging through the forest, toward no particular destination save anyplace as far from the trail as he could get.

Eventually exhaustion overwhelmed him and he collapsed to the forest floor, his entire left leg now swollen to twice its normal size. His pant leg had burst open at the seam. The area around the bite mark itself was bleeding and blistered, throbbing with razor-sharp pangs. The whole leg had turned an angry shade of purplish red. The small fire within his calf had now become an unholy conflagration consuming the entire left side of his body.

His heart, once having beaten so fast that he could feel it in his neck and ears, now rapidly slowed, his pulse dwindling until it was scarcely perceptible. His extremities turned ice-cold, yet his whole body was drenched with perspiration. He drifted in and out of consciousness for a brief period, and then, as night washed over the earth, succumbed fully to the venom.

IV. RISING FROM THE DEAD

There was only blackness, total blackness. His first thought was that he was somehow unconscious but able to think, however dimly and incoherently. He had never felt so groggy or disoriented in his life. He couldn't tell if he was standing or lying down. He wondered if he might simply be asleep, trapped in some vivid yet vacuous dream.

He thought: *My name is Alfred. Alfred Wilson Preston.*

Then, gradually, he became aware of three things: the first was an awful, steady throb in his right shoulder, as well as a queer numbness in his left calf. It felt as though a lead bearing had been planted in the tissue of his shoulder, pain fanning outward in pulsing rays. He winced, tried to grit his teeth but couldn't. His jaw was perfectly immobile. The second thing he noticed was how terribly *cold* he felt, as if he were trapped inside a block of ice. Yet he did not shiver at all. It was a biological paradox which confounded him, but which, in his groggy, addled state, he couldn't even venture to resolve. The third and final fact he now gleaned, which explained at least in part his arctic chill, was that he was utterly naked, razor-thin needles of ice clinging to his extremities.

He kept waiting for the darkness to dissipate, for his eyes to open and perceive some object, some shape or color. He would not be troubled if it were fuzzy and ill-defined, indeed, quite expected just that, for anything would so appear to a man emerging from a deep slumber.

Only it wasn't slumber. It was something far more extensive, far more profound. Were you in a coma? But what injury might have occasioned such a state? And why is there only silence as well as darkness? Why can't you hear anything, smell anything?

Except, slowly, he found he *could* smell something, something pungent and acrid, almost like bleach. Wherever he was, the air felt thin and sterile. Was he in a hospital? Surely not, as no bed could feel so stiff and rigid as whatever he lay on. At least now he was sufficiently oriented to discern that he was prostrate rather than erect.

He tried to move but couldn't. And then, for the first time realizing it consciously, he blinked, and thus discovered to his horror that his eyes *were* open. He was simply someplace utterly devoid of light.

He tried first to move his fingers, and then to wiggle his toes, and failed on both scores. Then he attempted to shift his head and found that he could, but just barely, perhaps by a fraction of an inch.

Memories came to him piecemeal, blurry but reachable, memories of being arrested at his house by Sheriff Caldwell and being escorted on horseback, toward the jailhouse in Gunphrey.

You didn't slip into a coma. You were simply unconscious, for God knows how long, and now you're finally coming to. But what happened to knock you out?

He strained his recollection, exerted himself to penetrate its depths, to excavate the memory he knew lay buried somewhere in its duskiest recess. But all he could call up was the faint image of storm clouds, and of the horse on which he'd ridden coming to a sudden halt. There had ensued general tumult thereafter. The Sheriff had been terribly agitated about something; the deputies had panicked; and Alfred...

You fled, he thought now, and then came a sudden, brilliant flash of recall: *You dashed up a hill, slid down another. The second was covered in frost, and then there was ice, a huge plane of it. It was a lake, the surface frozen over. There was a bird – a black bird, wasn't it, perhaps a sparrow? – alit on the far bank. It flew away, and then... and*

183

then you sat down upon a rock, didn't you? A big, craggy rock with sharp edges and deep cavities, rather like a meteor.

And then…

And then you were bitten. But by what? Some treacherous creature, it was. Some hideous, venomous fiend. A serpent, yes! 'Twas a serpent of the ugliest order. A viper! What kind of viper?

Now he whispered, "A Canadian water viper."

That he could speak at all amazed him, and galvanized him to test his limbs again. Now he discovered he could move his legs a bit, felt his feet brush against something solid, made, he thought, of iron or steel. He moved them in the other direction and again they bumped against a barrier of some sort, just as firm and unyielding. He twitched his arms, winced again at the pain in his shoulder, and tried to splay them. They moved in tiny increments, inch by arduous inch. And then, finally, encountered the same kind of surface as his feet had.

When, a few moments later, he was able to raise them slightly above his head, he felt a cold, damp ceiling. Now he squirmed about, endeavored to roll slightly to one side and then the other. He could only lift his right buttock about five degrees to the left before his shoulder collided with one of the walls. He did not dare repeat the experiment with his other buttock, terrified of the pain it would engender in his wounded shoulder when, inevitably, it met with the wall on the other side.

That was when Alfred realized he was trapped in a box of some kind, perhaps a coffin, or some supremely narrow compartment scarcely large enough to hold his body.

Good God, he thought, a sudden, frenzied trepidation stealing over him. *I've been buried alive.*

Racked with panic, and slowly regaining both his mental and bodily faculties, Alfred commenced to beat his feet and fists against the walls of whatever odious sepulcher confined him. His left leg felt heavy and ungainly, the numbness in his calf now giving way to spasmodic flares of thrumming pain. He cried for help in a hoarse, feeble voice he scarcely recognized as his own. But it was all to no avail. Surely nobody could hear him, and even if one were to, she would undoubtedly flee the scene in terror forthwith.

Pull it together, he thought now. *You must be calm in order to think clearly and logically. And so thinking is your only hope of escape. It's also what you do best, your very vocation. Every puzzle, every problem, be it empirical or logical, must admit of some solution. In which case your survival hinges on nothing more than devising a solution to* this *puzzle, to* this *problem.*

Only this, he feared, was neither a puzzle nor a problem to which logic, and far less mathematics, might be productively applied. It seemed a quandary, rather, much more akin to a terminal illness or being coerced into relinquishing one's billfold to a knife-wielding thief. A problem, in other words, admitting of only *one* solution: acceptance, resignation. Which in this instance meant certain death.

He took a deep breath of the thin air within which he lay, exhaled slowly. At some point his consternation subsided, giving way to a sort of hazy, reluctant fatalism and sheer exhaustion. Time seemed to stand still, to be almost irrelevant. If indeed he'd been buried or entombed alive, what good was time? It mattered only insofar as its passage would soon effect his demise, whether from asphyxiation, dehydration, starvation, or hypothermia.

And why *was* it so cold inside his claustrophobic prison? His nakedness notwithstanding, if he were buried under the earth, the temperature should be greater than that of the surface, which even at nighttime shouldn't be less than twenty or thirty degrees. Yet it felt to him as if the scarce air within his grave were almost sub-zero. A mausoleum or catacomb, both sheltered from the elements, should also feel much warmer. Thus, Alfred concluded, he was neither buried beneath the earth nor ensconced within an indoor tomb. So where, then, *was* he?

Deep Cold

The snakebite, he thought. *It caused a complete paralysis of all bodily functions, a catalepsy of sorts, save perhaps a very faint pulse and profoundly shallow respiration. A condition easily mistaken for clinical death. Just as happened with that Leonard Seymour chap in Burlington three years ago. The poor fellow was cut open on the autopsy table before the coroner realized he was still breathing, still alive. And if you're a fugitive suspected of cold-blooded murder, how carefully would those who discovered you, or even the coroner, bother to confirm your actual expiration?*

Within seconds, the whole picture became clear to him, and his location obvious: he was in a chamber, a cold chamber, inside an autopsy room. The doors to such chambers were locked, yes, but seldom by a deadbolt or furniture lock – seldom, that was, so securely as to resist considerable force. Far more likely, Alfred suspected, that it was fastened only by a padlock, and perhaps a weak one. An old, corroded one that might be rather easily sundered. After all, how steadfastly did the dead need to be stored?

But you can't be noticed, he thought. *You must find some way to escape the morgue undetected. You must be furtive, wily. You must marshal all the intellectual resources, all the cunning and stealth at your command.*

And so, very slowly, after ensuring that there was still no noise outside his chamber, Alfred began gently to press against its door, and then press harder, and harder still, until eventually he felt it begin to budge.

Finally, he held his breath and plowed his feet into it as forcefully but quietly as he could.

The lock snapped, and the door swung open.

There were three gurneys in the room, on two of which lay cadavers covered by stark white sheets. The third was bare and rusted, with a dark red stain on its upper left corner. Alfred surmised that this had been *his* gurney, and that the stain was that of blood from his shoulder, which still ached fiercely. He remembered now having been shot by either Caldwell or one of his deputies, supposed the bullet was still lodged in his muscle tissue. But he could not concern himself with that now, anymore than he could the terrible soreness in his left leg.

He half-limped, half-crept toward the door on the outer wall, listening for voices. At first he heard none, and then, rather distantly, that of a man. It was gruff but convivial, the words themselves inaudible. Then it drew closer, footsteps approaching the door, and Alfred heard the man say, "I suppose we'd ought to start on that Bancroft fellow if we're going to get out of here before midnight." Another male voice replied, "I'll join you in a moment, Frederick. I've just a few clerical items to attend to first."

A new panic bloomed in Alfred's chest, his breath catching in his throat. His mind raced at some terrific velocity. With scarcely a thought, he immediately turned and stood with his back against the wall, directly to the side of the door. He saw from the hinges that it would swing toward him once opened. He could only pray that Frederick wouldn't open it so widely that it collided with him. If it did, then it would be over, all of it, before he'd even a chance to escape.

Either by sheer good luck or divine providence, Frederick opened the door only halfway, just widely enough to enter. He moved blithely into the room, walked directly to the gurney farthest to his right - which was, fortuitously, opposite the side in which Alfred stood hiding. He waited a moment, until Frederick had pulled off the sheet and begun to inspect a wound in the corpse's neck, and then quietly, ever so quietly, slipped from behind the door and skulked out of the room, looking both ways before fully stepping out.

A long, brick corridor ran in both directions, the segment to his left lined with big oak doors and terminating at a stout granite wall. The segment to his right, much shorter, contained only a single door on the left and, at its end, a smallish partners desk facing the opposite wall. Upon the desk sat stacks of papers, a tall red candle, a wire basket, and an inkwell. Behind the desk, assiduously writing with a nib pen, sat a short, plump fellow of average frame with silver hair and a salt-and-pepper handlebar moustache. He wore a white doctor's coat, his plaid deerstalker cast to the side of the desk. A heavy sheepskin coat hung on a three-hook brass stand near the rear wall.

By virtue of yet another small miracle, directly ahead of Alfred was a short, empty hallway leading to the building's modest lobby – and, thus, to the exit. But what if there were someone minding the lobby, someone Alfred couldn't see, or a guard minding the outer door?

You've no choice but to try for it, he thought. *No choice but simply to hope the rest of the morgue is unmanned. And now, while that chap behind the desk is distracted, is your only chance to abscond. So go. Now.*

Alfred went, tip-toeing until he was clear of the coroner's view, and then stole almost silently toward the lobby. When he reached the end of the hallway he peeked around the corner and saw no one. He let out a hushed sigh of relief and quickly crossed the lobby to the door, the portal to his tenuous freedom.

He slowly turned the knob and opened it in minute measures, lest it creak. It did not. Once it was about a quarter open, he slipped sideways through the gap and into the bitter cold night, gently shutting the door behind him.

The town was dark and silent, not a soul stirring along the dimly lit street.

Nude as a newborn, his shoulder smarting viciously and teeth already beginning to chatter, Alfred Preston ducked into the shadows and made haste toward the edge of Timford.

V. ON THE LAM

He needed a plan, of course. And it would, by necessity, be a rather *elaborate* plan. First he must escape Timford before he was discovered missing from the morgue; then he must somehow disguise himself; then he must remain in hiding as much as possible; and then he must somehow exonerate himself before he could be re-arrested. The first three tasks seemed relatively easy by comparison to the fourth. He was a master of deduction, yes, but of detective work, of clandestine investigations and covert crime-solving, he knew next to nothing.

The key objective, of course, was to procure some hard evidence implicating at least Herman Gibbs, if not Gibbs and Caldwell both, in Julia's death. Only the most solid, tangible proof was likely to satisfy the law that someone other than Alfred himself was responsible for the crime, to clear his name convincingly and finally. But how to obtain such evidence, particularly when he was presumed dead and, if discovered alive, would once more become a wanted man? The whole endeavor seemed impossibly daunting. His only real advantage, he supposed, was that he undertook the mission in the dead of night, while the whole town slept, giving him (if he were lucky) at least a few hours to make himself scarce.

And so he pressed on, as discreetly but quickly as he could, shivering terribly from the cold and dimly aware that most of his body was growing numb. If he did not find shelter soon he would surely perish of frostbite. But he must keep moving. He must get out of the town –

Then he noticed a shop at the end of the street, darkened and undoubtedly locked, of course, but the sign above it faintly visible in the light from a nearby arc lamp: "MACARTHUR'S MEN'S SHOP."

He pressed his face against the picture window and peered inside, made out the rough outlines of suits and coats and hats. He reached gingerly for the doorknob, praying that it would turn freely in his hand, that somehow the shop owner had forgotten to lock up before leaving for the night. The knob did not budge, but held as fast as Alfred had feared and known it would. He felt like a man dying of thirst who had stumbled upon an oasis, only to discover a moment later that it was a mirage.

You need clothes, he thought. *You're going to die from the cold within an hour. The next town over is Walbrook, a good six miles from here. That's almost two hours on foot, even if you walk briskly, which is impossible with your injured shoulder and leg. And there are no horses about. You're going to have to break in somehow.*

He knew this thought was rational, indubitably correct. He knew in his logical mind that he must heed it, however risky and dismaying the enterprise. But for a moment fear held him back, fear of being detected. The tingling in his fingers and toes helped him quickly to squelch this fear, and, after taking a long, slow breath, he scoured the area for something with which he might break the glass.

He spotted a large rock lying near the storm drain at the street corner and scampered to retrieve it. He clenched his half-frozen fist around as much of it as he could, closed his eyes for a moment, opened them, and then hurled the rock at the glass next to the door of MacArthur's Men's Shop. The sound seemed to him to be deafening. And yet, when he looked about, turning frantically in every direction, he saw no shutters go up in the windows of the apartment houses on the opposite side of the street. He heard no voice cry out or door swing open, nobody calling for him to halt or any commotion of any kind. He heard nothing but the rustling of dead leaves blowing in the wind and, distantly, the hoot of an owl.

He carefully inserted his hand through the jagged hole in the glass, lifted the latch on the back-plate, and turned the knob.

He crept inside and closed the door behind him, his heart racing again, most of the feeling in his hands and feet gone now, his skin caked with frost.

He fumbled about in the dark until he came up with a pair of long johns, a pair of trousers, a burgundy wool jumper, an overcoat, a pair of black cotton socks, some leather boots (not exactly a perfect fit, but they would do), a brown felt top hat, and, best of all, a large black wig that completely covered his sandy brown hair. The hair of the wig was curly, unruly, his own flat and straight. It was a perfect contrast.

He spied the cash register on the counter and thought about trying to break into it, but decided he hadn't adequate time. Besides, the proprietor would have surely removed all the cash and stored it in the vault before locking up for the night.

Alfred nearly left before noticing a small shelf with false moustaches and beards, of all sizes and varieties and colors. He chose a black horseshoe moustache and a pair of bushy mutton chops to match the wig, affixed them quickly, and slunk out of the store.

Fully dressed now, and slowly warming up, he made his way toward Walbrook, hoping he could find a place to sleep once he got there.

The pain in his shoulder grew worse.

*　　*　　*

He arrived in Walbrook just before dawn. The town's sole inn looked almost deserted, its door illuminated by a single gas lamp.

Alfred went inside, trying to disguise his stiff gait and stifle the pain in his shoulder. The innkeeper sat behind a long pine desk with a lantern on one side. Two candelabras otherwise illuminated the vestibule.

"May I help you?" asked the innkeeper. He was a gaunt, elderly man with deep furrows in his brow, a pair of wire-rimmed spectacles resting low on his bulbous nose.

"I certainly hope so," said Alfred, making his voice sound as plaintive as he could. It wasn't difficult. "I'm afraid my horse and billfold were purloined early this morning, and now I'm rather abandoned here in Walbrook. I'm on my way to Middletown. I walked here from Timford, in the freezing cold, as I knew this was the nearest hotel. I'm desperately tired, sir, and chilled to the bone. I've no means to rent a room, but am asking for your mercy. I can make arrangements with an associate to send payment by this evening, I assure you, if you'll only let me have a bed for a few hours."

The innkeeper leaned back in his chair and appraised him at length, as if debating whether to swallow this rather outlandish tale of woe. Eventually he said, "You're fortunate, Mister, that I'm a good Christian with benevolent tendencies. I was raised to take pity on those in a hard spot."

"Oh, sir, I can't tell you how grateful -"

"But I also wasn't raised to be a fool so that tricksters and swindlers could take advantage of my charity. I'm also a businessman, my humanitarian instincts aside. This inn is how I make my living, and without charging my tenants, I couldn't afford to feed myself or my family. You understand?"

"Entirely, Mister...?"

"Stockton. And you are?"

"Brummond," said Alfred. "Stanley Brummond." He tipped his hat. "A pleasure to meet you, sir."

The innkeeper nodded. "Likewise, Mr. Brummond. Of German descent, are you?"

"Second-generation American, yes."

"My great-grandmother was German."

"Oh?"

"Yes. From Heidelberg. She lived to be a ninety-two, as a matter of fact."

"That's remarkable."

Mr. Stockton nodded again, leaned forward. "So here's what: I'll let you have a room for eight hours, and give you till six this evening to make good on it. I won't charge you any extra – the rate for a standard room is thirty-five cents per night - but if the money isn't in my hands by six, I'll report you to the town sheriff and have a warrant issued for your arrest. Is that a fair deal, Mr. Brummond?"

Reluctantly, Alfred nodded. "Seems eminently fair to me, sir."

"Very good, then."

Mr. Stockton reached into a desk drawer and removed a key, handed it to Alfred. "Go up the stairs and turn left down the hallway. It'll be the second room on your right."

Alfred tipped his hat again and thanked the gentleman profusely, made his way up the stairs and down the hallway and into the room.

He hung his wig on a hook beside the door and undressed, then got into the small bed and pulled the sheets up over his body, savoring the warmth. He was asleep within five minutes.

*   *   *

He awoke six hours later, his shoulder so stiff and sore he could hardly bend his right arm. He winced, yawned, rubbed sleep from his eyes with the knuckles on his left hand, and gently swung his feet onto the floor. He felt rested but disoriented, the events of the previous day seeming now quite incredible, almost dreamlike. He dressed slowly, methodically, sliding his right arm through the sleeves of his jumper and coat with great care. He had not bothered to remove his fake moustache or beard before going to sleep, and now looked in the mirror atop the dresser to make sure they had not come loose or fallen crooked. Though the skin beneath them itched badly, they remained securely in place.

He donned his wig and went downstairs, where an old woman with gray hair and bifocals sat behind the innkeeper's desk. Alfred presumed she was Mr. Stockton's wife.

"You the fella who owes us thirty-five cents for the room?" she asked him ill-humoredly. Apparently she did not share her husband's proclivity for kindliness.

"I am," Alfred said, stepping toward the desk. "And I promised your husband – I presume he was your husband, anyhow – that I'd have the money to him by six o' clock this evening."

She glanced at a grandfather clock standing against the wall by the door. "That gives you about seven hours," she said.

"I shouldn't require that much time."

She nodded briskly and bade him good day.

VI. A TELEGRAM TO THOMAS

There was a Western Union office on the corner. Alfred went inside, jingling a bell on the door, and walked up to the counter. A portly fellow with a moustache not unlike Alfred's false one greeted him with a nod. He sat behind a window with a half-moon opening at the bottom. "May I help you?" he asked.

"I certainly hope so," Alfred said. "I'm in a bit of a sticky situation, you see."

"Oh? How's that?"

"I've no money, I'm afraid, as my billfold was filched by a pickpocket this morning, who seems also to have made off with my horse. I'm en route to Middletown and desperately need to get in touch with a fellow who resides in Timford. He has access to all my funds and assets, and could furnish me with plenty of money to purchase a new horse and finance the remainder of my journey."

"And you want the money sent by courier, I presume?"

"Indeed. But of course, first I must find some way to pay for the telegram, that I might reach him with my request. Once received, he could pay the fee to have the money sent by courier, and then I could simply retrieve it here. And I rather need it in a hurry, as I've a debt to pay the innkeeper for lodging last night."

The man behind the counter appeared to mull all this over. "I understand your situation, sir, and quite sympathize with it, but I'm afraid I can't send a telegram on your behalf without charging you for it."

"Of course not," said Alfred. "But perhaps we could barter?"

"What have you to offer?"

Alfred glanced down at his overcoat, tugged on the flaps. "How about this? I paid four dollars for it. How much do you charge for an expedited telegram?"

"One-fifty," said the man. "Provided it's forty words or fewer."

Alfred sighed, as if reluctant to make the bargain. "I'll let you have the coat for the telegram and ask for nothing in return."

The telegrapher told Alfred to come closer, inspected the coat at length. It was, naturally, in mint condition. "That deal seems fair to me," he said.

"Wonderful."

The man turned to his telegraph machine and depressed the key. "To whom is the telegram to be addressed?"

"Thomas Usher," said Alfred.

The telegrapher tapped the key a few times. "Street address?"

Reluctantly, Alfred gave his home address. He waited with clenched teeth for the telegrapher to say that the address sounded familiar, to raise some quarrel about the matter. But he simply tapped his key again and carried on.

"And the message?"

"Please courier five hundred dollars to Western Union office in Walbrook immediately. Go to WU office in Framingham. Matter extremely urgent. Also, do not empty the kitchen garbage."

The telegrapher had been tapping away at the key rather nonchalantly and now stopped abruptly. "I'm sorry," he said. "'Don't empty the kitchen garbage?'"

"Yes, that's right. I believe I may have unintentionally disposed of something valuable."

The telegrapher shook his head, as if to say, *I've heard it all now.* "And the name of the sender?"

"Just the initials 'A.P.'," said Alfred, "will suffice."

The money arrived four hours later, a period which to Alfred had felt like an eternity. If the messenger had encountered Caldwell or any of his deputies along the way, or reported any suspicions to the police, Alfred supposed he would already be in jail. That the transaction had been successfully effected

Michael Prescott

signified, therefore, that, at least for the time being, all was well. Probably Caldwell and his boys were too busy investigating the morgue and MacArthur's Men's Shop to have anyone deployed at the estate.

Alfred filled out the form necessary to collect the money, and the gentleman to whom he'd relinquished his coat thanked him for his business.

"The pleasure was all mine," Alfred replied. He turned to leave, then hesitated. He looked back at the telegrapher. "Say, you wouldn't happen to know where I could find the nearest horse breeder, would you? Or anyone who might be willing to sell a horse of his own?

The telegrapher pondered for a moment. "I believe there's a horse farm over in Bainbridge," he said. "That's about five miles east of here, if you don't know the area."

"I do," Alfred said. "And would you happen to know also if there's a doctor in Bainbridge?"

"I believe there is, yes."

209

"Excellent. Have a lovely day, sir."

"And you."

Alfred left the office, returned to the inn, and made good on his debt. Mr. Stockton told him that men like Alfred were proof that there were still decent, honest souls in the world, despite his wife's cynical insistence to the contrary. Alfred chuckled, thanked him for his hospitality, and bade him well wishes.

He bought a heavy, second-hand coat from a tailor's shop and made his way through town, avoiding eye contact with passers-by. Then he set out toward Bainbridge, using the sun as his guide, trying his best to ignore the mounting pain in his shoulder.

VII. A DOCTOR AND A HORSE

He arrived in Bainbridge at dusk, exhausted from the journey. He found the nearest hotel, paid in cash for a room, and slept till dawn.

Next morning he visited the doctor's office at the other end of town. It was a small outfit staffed by a single physician and a nurse who appeared to double as a receptionist. A plain, petite woman with long eyelashes, she asked how she might be of assistance.

"I've a bullet wound," he told her. "Actually, a bullet lodged in my right shoulder."

"Oh, dear! How on earth did *that* happen?"

"A hunting accident," he said (quite convincingly, he thought). "My friend and I were hunting quail when he dropped his rifle and caused it to fire. It wasn't at close range, thankfully, but the bullet is nevertheless lodged quite deeply."

"Let me summon the doctor," she said, rising from her chair.

"Thank you."

The doctor, a spindling man with large, misshapen ears, appeared a moment later and gestured for Alfred to follow him back to the examination room.

"Sit up on the table and remove your jumper, please," the doctor said. He was apparently not one for formalities.

Alfred did as he was instructed.

"My God!" the doctor gasped, inspecting the entry wound. "When did this occur?"

"Two days ago," Alfred said.

"And why didn't you seek medical attention immediately?"

Alfred had expected this question and was prepared for it. "I did," he said, "but the doctor I consulted told me he was ill-equipped to deal with it. He hadn't the necessary implements. His is an even smaller practice than yours."

"Which doctor is this?"

"Lindbergh," said Alfred. "Hans Lindbergh. From Mapleton. That's where I'm from."

"I've never heard of him."

"I believe he's new to the trade."

"Well," said the doctor, "anyhow, let's first disinfect the wound with phenol and then administer some ether."

"All right."

The doctor started toward a cabinet across the room, then halted in mid-stride. "I'll charge twelve dollars and fifty cents for this procedure. Can you afford that amount?"

"I can. But before we begin, there's another matter, perhaps equally urgent, which needs attending to."

The doctor arched his eyebrows. "Oh? And what might that be?"

Alfred rolled up his left pant leg and showed his wound to the doctor. "After I was shot, I was bitten by a snake. A venomous one, I believe."

"Jesus wept!" exclaimed the doctor, coming over to examine the bite mark and attendant trauma. "That's one hell of a day you had there, I'd say."

"Some men are just unlucky, I suppose. I've reduced the swelling a good bit with ice, however. I could barely fit into my trousers yesterday."

"Were you in extreme cold at time of the bite and for a prolonged period thereafter? That's the only medical explanation for how the venom wouldn't have killed you. Extreme cold would have largely shut down your circulatory system so as to preclude the venom from reaching your heart."

"As a matter of fact I was," Alfred said. "My friend and I were on foot, and the morning was dreadfully cold. It took him nearly an hour to carry me back to his horse."

"No," said the doctor. "An hour wouldn't have been long enough. I daresay your survival, sir, was something of a miracle, or else a profound medical mystery."

Alfred smiled weakly. "Perhaps, then," he said, "I'm not as unlucky as I'd thought."

"Perhaps not." The doctor lit a stove match and held it close to the wound, prying at it with his other hand. "Does that cause you any soreness? Is the muscle tissue tender?"

Alfred winced. "Yes," he said. "Quite."

"That's good," said the doctor. "That means necrosis hasn't yet set in."

"Necrosis?"

The doctor patted him on the shoulder. "You won't lose the leg," he said. "But to treat the leg wound as well, I'll have to charge you an additional eight dollars."

Alfred nodded. "That's a fair price, Doctor. Just so long as I'll be mobile."

"Oh, you'll be perfectly mobile. But don't expect to run any marathons in the next few months."

Alfred smiled. "I'll be content," he said, "with evening strolls."

He purchased a mare from the farmer, a fellow by the name of John Reynolds, for the price of sixty-five dollars. She was young and healthy, with a lovely coat of sheen, copper hair. Her name was Lucy. She was already broken-in and well trained, heeding his commands as if he had owned her his whole life. She rather reminded Alfred of Samantha, about whose welfare he worried nearly as much as he did that of his servants.

He rode Lucy for about twenty-five miles, until he reached the fairly large town of Cricksville. Once there, he found a hitching post outside the general store and dismounted the mare, tying her reins to the post. He went into the store and bought various foodstuffs and a cheap billfold, along with a knapsack in which to store the goods. He deposited the remainder of his money into the billfold, draped the knapsack over his good shoulder, and then walked across the street to a boarding house.

The interior of the place was quite bare, with only sparse furnishings. A scrawny, youngish man in suspenders, sporting a goatee and a cowboy hat, sat in a Brewster chair, puffing away on a corncob pipe. The whole room smelled of tobacco smoke. He removed the pipe from his mouth just long enough to ask whether Alfred wished to rent a room.

"I do," Alfred said, extending his hand. "Jacob Barlow, from Platt Valley."

"By the week or by the month?" asked the hayseed from his chair, making no effort to get up, much less to shake Alfred's hand.

Alfred lowered his hand, trying not to grimace in pain. "What are your rates?"

"Four per week," said the hayseed. "Thirteen-fifty per month. Unless you're lookin' for, uh, superior accommodations?"

Alfred shook his head. "Standard accommodations will be fine, thank you. And a week, then. At least to start."

"Cash money only," the fellow said, standing at last. "No checks, no trades."

"I have cash."

The hayseed went over to a cash register on an L-shaped counter and pulled a lever to spring open the drawer. He set his pipe in a bronze ashtray. "Four greenbacks," he muttered.

Alfred produced the money from his new billfold and tendered it to the toothpick in suspenders. "There you are," he said.

The hayseed plucked a key from a rack behind the counter and handed it to Alfred. "It's number eight. Third floor. Last door on your left."

"Thank you, sir." He began to turn away.

"Your name again?"

He turned back, gave the hayseed a big, toothy grin. "Jacob. Jacob Barlow."

"Got it." The young man jotted the name down in a ledger and went back to smoking his pipe.

VIII. CALDWELL ON THE HUNT

Alfred took dinner at a restaurant next to the general store. He'd asked the store owner's permission to leave Lucy hitched to the post until after he'd eaten, which permission the owner had happily granted. Alfred feasted on roasted lamb, scalloped potatoes, and green beans, the first substantial meal he'd consumed in three days. He also ordered two snifters of brandy, mostly to alleviate the pain in his shoulder. The doctor in Bainbridge had done a fine job of removing the bullet and stitching the wound, but the soreness, he'd advised, would persist for weeks.

He paid for his meal and left the restaurant. As he approached Lucy, who appeared to be asleep, a crossing gust blew a newspaper against his feet, the pages rattling against his boots. He bent down and gathered it up, piecing the pages back together. It was a copy of the *Sanford County Dispatch* from the previous day. The street was brightly illuminated by a moonlight tower erected near the edge of town, and in its harsh white glare Alfred read the paper's headline:

BODY OF SUSPECTED MURDERER

MISSING FROM TIMFORD MORGUE;

MEN'S CLOTHING STORE

BURGLARIZED

Alfred quickly stuffed the newspaper into his coat, fastening the top three buttons, and went to unhitch Lucy from the post outside the store. He walked her over to a post on the porch of the boarding house, re-hitched her, and went inside.

Nobody was in the lobby. The Brewster chair sat empty, the counter abandoned. The only sign of life was the pervasive smell of cherry-flavored pipe tobacco (a rather significant improvement, Alfred thought, over the previous odor).

Alfred made haste for the stairs, climbed them, and hurried to his room. He closed and locked the door behind him, then fished a book of matches from his coat pocket and lit the two candles over the bed. After tossing his wig on the nightstand, he unbuttoned his coat and carried the newspaper over to the desk in the corner. He lit the candle that sat off to the side and sunk into the chair, spreading the newspaper open upon the desk. He read, with both great alarm and intense curiosity, the article at the top of page one:

TIMFORD, CT - The body of Alfred Wilson Preston, the esteemed logician and professor of Timford, Connecticut who on Tuesday was arrested for the murder of his wife, has apparently gone missing from the town's morgue. The absence of Dr. Preston's body was discovered by Frederick Amsel, a coroner at the morgue, approximately twelve hours after the remains had been received.

Martin Foster, Mr. Amsel's colleague, told the Dispatch that he himself had placed Dr. Preston's body in a cold chamber within an hour of its arrival, and that the chamber had been secured in typical fashion. The disappearance of Dr. Preston's body was discerned only when Mr. Amsel noticed that the lock on the cold chamber had been broken.

"It's quite inexplicable," said Mr. Amsel during a brief interview. "There are only two possibilities, equally absurd: the first is that somebody surreptitiously snapped the lock and stole off with the body without being detected; the second is that Mr. Preston was somehow still alive and actually managed to escape both the chamber and the morgue under his own power."

On the evening of February 3rd, Dr. Preston escaped while being transported to the county jail after a snake apparently spooked the horses on which the Sheriff, his deputies, and Dr. Preston were riding. The Sheriff and his deputies opened fire on Dr. Preston as he fled through a field, and it is believed that at least one bullet struck him. He was later found, presumably dead of a snakebite, upon the floor of a dense forest, approximately three miles from the trail.

Meanwhile, MacArthur's Men's Shop, located just a short distance from Timford's morgue, was burglarized in the pre-dawn hours of February 4th. Various garments and sundry accessories were reported missing, including a black wig and a false moustache and mutton chops of matching color. Authorities in Timford suspect a connection between the two incidents but have not as yet completed their investigation of the latter.

Any persons with information concerning the whereabouts of Dr. Preston or his remains, or the burglary of MacArthur's Men Shop, are commanded to contact the Sanford County Sheriff's Department forthwith, on pain of criminal charges.

A rather fuzzy photograph of Alfred taken a year or two earlier had been printed beneath the article.

Alfred read it twice, then folded the newspaper in half and hid it under his mattress. He would need to alter his appearance early the next day, feared that the hayseed or the proprietor of the general store or even the waiter at the restaurant might have already reported their encounters with him to Caldwell. But if that were the case, he assured himself, he would have already been re-arrested and transported to the jailhouse in Gunphrey.

And then, as he began to disrobe, he realized that an obvious but crucial fact had long escaped him: *If you're dead, your nephew will inherit your estate. Neither Caldwell nor Gibbs will be able to touch it. Thus Caldwell will summon all the resources at his disposal to prove you're still alive, to locate you and return you to his custody. But unless he does, there can be no auction of your estate. Nor, until your death is confirmed, can the estate and your assets be subject to probate. Hence everything will remain in limbo until and unless you're found alive.*

This, of course, meant he had more time than he'd originally supposed, more time to devise a plan by which to both prove his innocence and preserve his property. So long, that was, as he was careful. And careful he would be.

I want him alive! he now heard Sheriff Caldwell shouting in his memory. *Do you understand me? I want that man taken alive!*

Alfred smiled as he climbed into bed. *Yes,* he thought. *Of course you want me alive, you son of a bitch. And when at last I show you that I am, it will be down upon you, not I, whom the righteous and heavy hand of justice is brought squarely.*

IX. DRESSING LIKE THE ENEMY

The trip to Middletown took a day and a half. The first night he'd camped in an open field, tying Lucy to the trunk of a tall dogwood. He'd slept in a one-man tent he'd bought in a town twenty miles north of

Cricksville, outside Sanford County. He had built a small fire with kindling he'd gathered from a forest floor, roasted some rabbit meat and red bell peppers.

Alfred now hitched Lucy to a post outside the Middletown County Courthouse and then made his way into the State Police Barracks. He had since shaved his head completely before buying a dark brown wig, a pair of clear-lens spectacles, and a false chestnut beard about nine inches in length. He had also purchased a used Sholes & Glidden typewriter and a variety of hairpins, the latter stashed presently in a paper sack in the breast pocket of his coat. He carried a tan leather briefcase in his left hand. A week had passed since he'd left Cricksville and taken up residence at a boarding house on the outskirts of Danbury.

He now went directly downstairs, to the washroom, which was adjacent to the locker room in which the officers stored their uniforms, badges, helmets, and weapons. He entered one of the stalls, latched the door, and waited patiently, until, about twenty minutes later, he heard footsteps coming down the stairs. He held his breath for a moment, keeping perfectly still, prepared merely to utter the word "occupied" in a low voice should the individual attempt to open the stall door.

But he did not. He continued, instead, into the locker room. Alfred got on his hands and knees and peered through the gap between the floor and the side of the stall, watched in delight as a constable unfastened his badge, removed his helmet and uniform, and placed the apparel into one of the lockers, along with his baton and side arm. He changed into his civilian garbs, slid the shackle of a padlock through a loop in the locker door, secured it, and, whistling, walked briskly out of the locker room and back up the stairs.

Now Alfred moved quickly, ever so quickly. He dashed to the locker in question, yanked the bag of hairpins from his pocket, and pulled one out. He inserted it into the keyhole of the padlock, twisted it gently this way and that, listened for a click and heard nothing. He then tried another pin and got the same result. A third pin did the trick, and with terrific haste

Alfred swung open the door and began to collect the constable's belongings. Then he heard more footsteps on the stairs.

The items in hand, he raced back to the stall, threw the latch, and hunkered down on the commode, breathing heavily but quietly. After the officer did his business, Alfred quickly undressed and examined the constable's helmet and badge. The wreath insignia on the helmet bore the constable's name, rank, and precinct number, while his badge was embossed only with his precinct and division numbers. He made sure the helmet was a reasonable fit and then, a plan in mind, quickly changed into the constable's uniform, pinning the badge to the shirt and holstering the side arm and baton. Holding the helmet in one hand, he picked up his briefcase with the other. He opened the stall door quietly, looked about, and, mustering all the aplomb he could manage, headed up the stairs.

The hallway was empty. He paced leisurely through it, scanning the stenciled lettering on the various doors until he located a clerk's office. He knocked on the door and a female voice invited him to enter.

He donned the helmet, opened the door, and stepped into the office.

"Good afternoon," he said in a pleasant, even tone, at once removing his helmet and favoring the secretary with a slight bow.

Behind a narrow desk sat a roundish, towheaded woman with her hair curled on top and taken into a bun at the back, a single golden ringlet dangling over her shoulder. "Good afternoon," she said, frowning slightly. "May I help you, Officer?"

"Yes," he said. "I'm a new constable here, was hired on this morning. I was drafted from a department in Boston. My name's Henry Clayton. It's a pleasure to meet you, Ms. Franklin." He manufactured his most artful, beguiling smile.

"I didn't hear anything about our hiring a new constable," she said, creasing her brow. "But it's always nice to see a new face around here."

"And it's always a delight to see a face so comely as yours, if I may say so, Ms. Franklin."

She blushed, finally smiling a bit. "That's very kind of you. So, what can I do for you, Officer Clayton? Or did you merely come to introduce yourself?"

He opened his briefcase and produced two documents of legal size. "I simply need two letters notarized and marked as State Police correspondence, please. And two envelopes bearing the address of the Barracks."

"Certainly," said the clerk.

Please don't read them, Alfred thought (or prayed, really). *Please don't even glance at them.*

She didn't. She simply pressed two wafer seals onto their top right corners, stamped them with dark blue ink at the bottom, and handed the letters back to him. Then she reached into a basket and sifted out two envelopes, extending them across the desk. He took them and thanked her very much for her help.

"Anytime," she said. "Would you like me to mail them for you? I've an outgoing basket right here."

Alfred shook his head. "That's all right, Ms. Franklin. As it happens, I'm on my way to the post office now. But thank you, all the same." He stuffed the letters and envelopes into his briefcase, fastened it, and started toward the door.

And then he heard her voice from behind him: "Oh, Officer Clayton?"

His heart took a giant leap, tried to squeeze its way into his throat. He turned around slowly, on feet made of lead, endeavoring to mask the trepidation in his features. "Yes, Ms. Franklin?"

"Welcome to the Force," she said, smiling broadly.

He nearly shuddered with relief, smiling back at her. "Thank you, ma'am. I'm delighted to be a part of it." He gave her another small bow and hastily exited her office, closing the door behind him.

Keeping his head down, he strode quickly down the hall and out the building, back to the courthouse, where he unhitched Lucy and set off immediately for Danbury.

X. LOOKING FOR LEADS

Three days later, he made a trip to a pharmacy in Pookskill, about eleven miles southwest of Bainbridge. The pharmacy was a small establishment, but by appearances well patronized. Old gents and blue-haired biddies roamed the aisles, searching for ointments and cough syrups and laxatives. Middle-aged men were stocking up on hair tonic and shaving soap, young ladies on perfumes and face powder. A horde of giddy children stood before the sweets counter, ogling sundry confections: chocolate malt balls and caramel toffees, jelly beans and peppermints. Two teenage boys stood beside a soda fountain, joking and laughing.

Alfred, fully disguised, went back to the druggist's counter and found a tall, broad-shouldered fellow in a white coat, filling bottles with various liquids and tablets. He wore spectacles with tortoise-shell frames and had jet-black hair parted straight down the middle, combed flat on both sides. Doctors' prescriptions were held with clothes pegs along a string spanning the length of the lab. As the druggist was plugging one of the bottles with a cork, Alfred signaled for his attention and apologized for the interruption.

"Pardon me," Alfred said, "but I seem to be vexed by a rather nasty vermin problem at my home. Rats, specifically. I was hoping to procure some sort of poison with which to be rid of them. Have you any suggestions?"

The druggist set the bottle down and approached the counter. He appeared both cautious and thoughtful. "Well," he said, "there's strychnine, which comes in various brand-names, like Certox and Sanaseed. And then of course there's arsenic, which you can find in just about any household box of rat poison, or arsenide compounds to make your own poison at home. Those are the only two rodenticides currently on the market of which *I'm* aware. But the sale of both is heavily regulated by the government these days – the big boys in Washington, I mean, the ones that like to meddle in businesses they don't understand – so a druggist needs a special license in order to sell them. And he must keep meticulous, detailed records of all sales of such products, as well. The licensing fee is expensive, and the record-keeping quite onerous, so the number of druggists who even bother to carry or produce such items anymore is swiftly dwindling."

"Oh," Alfred said, feigning surprise and disappointment. In fact he'd done considerable research on the subject at the library in Danbury, was already well aware of the restrictions on the sale of such toxicants. "So I gather, then, that you're not among those who still do?"

The druggist shook his head regretfully. "I'm afraid not, sir. I just fill doctors' prescriptions and sell what I can over the counter, none of which would be of much use to you, except maybe as bait with which to combine the poison."

"Such as?"

"Honey, say, or flour. Those are the most typical ingredients in an arsenide compound."

Alfred nodded. "I see. So are you aware of any druggist in the area who *is* licensed to sell these poisons?"

The druggist frowned. "I'm afraid you'll have to make quite a journey if you want anything like that," he said. "To my knowledge, there's only one druggist in the whole state of Connecticut who still manufactures strychnine and arsenide compounds, and he's all the way in Bridgeport. I don't know whether he vends boxes of rat poison itself, though."

"Ah," said Alfred. "Would you happen to know his name?"

The druggist scratched his chin, shifting his eyes up and to the left. "Jensen, I believe. Kyle Jensen."

"Thank you," Alfred said, and turned to leave.

"Sir?"

A flutter of fear ran through him, much like his sudden dread at the State Police Barracks when Ms. Franklin had called him back. He turned around to face the druggist. "Yes?"

"Have you tried applying wet Lye around the edges of the rat holes? I do carry *that*."

"Of course," Alfred said, his heart slowing and stomach settling into place. "No good. They just chew new ones."

"Oh," said the druggist, giving a shrug. "Rats."

*   *   *

It was a sixty-mile trip to Bridgeport across largely rough terrain. Toward the end Lucy began to whinny in protest, but Alfred was determined to reach the city by nightfall and so whipped her lightly with a crop to keep her moving at a steady trot. Once arrived, he hitched her to a post outside a large, rather fancy hotel downtown. He checked in under the name Charles Beaucamp.

Next day, he dressed in the constable's uniform he'd swiped in Middletown, affixed his badge and disguise, and walked four blocks to the city courthouse. He carried his briefcase in his left hand and an envelope in his right. He went inside and walked up three flights of stairs, to the Circuit Clerk's Office. A shapely woman in an orange-and-gold princess-line dress sat behind one of the glass windows. He went to her, bade her good morning, set his briefcase on the floor, and handed her the envelope. It was addressed to Judge Leonard Hobbes of Connecticut's Ninth Judicial Circuit. The return address was that of the Middletown State Police Barracks.

"It's a request for a subpoena," Alfred said. "The matter is rather urgent, so I was asked to hand-deliver the letter myself."

She glanced at the return address on the envelope, then back at Alfred. "You're an officer with the State Police Department?"

"Yes, ma'am, that's right. Officer Henry Clayton of Middletown." He pointed to his badge.

"I see." She opened the envelope, removed the letter, and examined it, noting the seal at the top and the stamp at the bottom. She scanned the content quickly, then looked up at Alfred. "I'll pass this along to Judge Hobbes," she said. "He's presiding over a trial right now, but the session shouldn't last too much longer."

"Is there any other judge available to sign it? It needn't be Judge Hobbes."

She considered. "Well, Judge Wolcott may have a spare moment. Let me check with his secretary."

"Very well."

The clerk picked up a speaking-tube and called for the secretary. A moment later the clerk said, "Yes, hello, Milicent, how are you? Lucille here. I've an officer from the State Police in Middletown with a request for a subpoena. The letter is addressed to Judge Hobbes, but he's in trial at the moment and the officer tells me any judge's signature will do. Would Judge Wolcott have a few minutes to review the request?" Short pause, then: "He would? Oh, that's fine. I'll send it down now. Thank you, Millie."

The clerk folded the letter, placed it back in the envelope, and dropped it through a tube jutting up from the floor. The tube was labeled "Ms. Johnson – Judge Wolcott." Then she turned back to Alfred. "It shouldn't be too long," she said.

"That's fine. I'll just have a seat and wait. Thank you much for your help, ma'am."

"Gladly, Officer."

Alfred took a seat against the wall, drawing the briefcase into his lap. He forced himself to keep still and composed. He was worried the judge might ask to confer with him, so as to elicit more details concerning the subject matter of the request. But then, about ten minutes later, a messenger boy came through the door and delivered a document to the clerk. It was the subpoena, signed by Judge Wolcott.

The clerk waved him forward. "Officer Clayton, was it?"

"Yes," Alfred said, standing.

"Your subpoena's signed and ready."

"Excellent." He walked casually to the window and opened his briefcase.

"Would you like that in an envelope?"

"Yes, please."

The clerk slid the subpoena into an envelope bearing the address of the Fairfield County Courthouse, licked the seal, and pressed the flap down. "There you are, Officer."

"Thank you, ma'am." He put the letter inside his briefcase, fastened the snaps, and tipped his constable's hat to the clerk, smiling affably. "You've been of great assistance."

"Of course. Have a pleasant day, Officer."

"Likewise."

He left the courthouse quickly, unhitched Lucy, and rode the mile and a half to the Jensen Pharmacy and Emporium on Barkley Street.

XI. THE LEDGER AND THE LETTER

It was a much larger outfit than the pharmacy in Pookskill. It had not one but *three* soda fountains, and two display cases full of candies rather than just one. It also had four times as many aisles, with four times as many products for sale. Today was Saturday, and if the Pookskill pharmacy had been crowded, then Jensen's was perfectly *packed*.

The druggist's counter was situated at the front of the emporium. There were two men in white smocks behind the counter, one filling prescriptions and the other entering information into a ledger. Alfred went to the latter fellow and asked if he was Kyle Jensen.

"I am," admitted the druggist reluctantly. "Are you a police officer?"

"Yes, sir, I am. I'm with the Connecticut State Police, out of Middletown. My name is Henry Clayton."

Now the druggist stood, fear penetrating his eyes. His colleague had ceased filling bottles and now simply stood there, looking on with dismay and bewilderment. "Am I in some kind of trouble, Officer?"

"No," said Alfred. "*You're* not in any trouble, but I'm afraid one of your customers may be. I have a subpoena here." Now he opened his briefcase and produced the document, handed it over to Jensen. "It's come to our attention, sir, that a certain fellow by the name of Herman Gibbs, of Timford in Sanford County, routinely does business with your emporium. That, to wit, he purchases on a regular basis either rat poison containing arsenic or else arsenide compounds. Do you recognize his name?"

Jensen nodded, his face now three shades paler. His jaw slackened and eyes widened as he skimmed the subpoena. "I... I believe so, yes. He runs a general store out there in Timford, does he not?"

"He does. And do you sell any arsenic-laden products here in your pharmacy?"

"We've a few brands of rodent poisons with arsenic in them, yes. Rat Begone, Mouse-Rid, Vermin No More. But Mr. Gibbs has always ordered the arsenide compounds."

Alfred crossed his arms over his chest, maintaining a grave and authoritative disposition. "Yes, we suspected as much."

"He has them delivered by courier about twice a month. It's been a while since his last order, though. I simply assumed he'd no longer any use for them, that the vermin plaguing his store had finally been disposed of."

Alfred nodded impatiently. "Yes, well, as you can see from the subpoena, I'll need copies of all bills of sale associated with such purchases by Mr. Gibbs or any of his employees or associates. I'll also need to confiscate your ledger, I'm afraid."

"Yes, Officer, of course. That won't be a problem at all. Just give me a few moments to locate the bills of sale, if that's all right."

"There's no great hurry, Mr. Jensen. Just don't dawdle, please."

"Of course not."

The druggist started toward the back of the lab and then turned around, his face awash with apprehension. "You're certain I'm not in any sort of trouble, right, Officer? I mean, I have a license to sell -"

"Relax, Mr. Jensen. I told you that you're not under any suspicion and I meant what I said. The extent of your involvement in this matter will be to comply with this subpoena and perhaps, at a later date, to answer a few questions and be called to testify at Mr. Gibbs's trial, provided he's even arrested. This investigation is still in its early stages, and I'm not at liberty to disclose any further details. But rest assured that you won't be prosecuted for anything unless you've broken some law."

"I haven't," Jensen insisted.

Alfred raised his hands, palms outward. "Then you've nothing to worry about. Now, the bills of sale, please?"

"Back in a jiffy," Jensen said, and disappeared into a back room.

Deep Cold

*   *   *

Alfred returned to his boarding house in
Danbury, where he was paying by the week. He gave a
nod to the owner as he entered the dwelling and
plodded up the stairs to his room. He was exhausted,
but still had a couple of tasks to attend to before going
to bed.

He carried his briefcase over to the writing desk
in the corner, opened his briefcase, and removed the
ledger he'd seized from Jensen's Pharmacy and
Emporium. There were in all a dozen entries for orders
by Herman Gibbs's General Store, scattered between
orders by other merchants and purchases by individual
patrons (mostly for boxes of rat and mouse poison).
Gibbs's orders appeared on six separate sheets, the first
transaction dating back to August of 1885. Before
departing Jensen's, Alfred had purchased a fountain
pen filled with red ink. He now went through the ledger
and circled each of the entries pertaining to Gibbs, the
first three of which read:

246

DATE	ITEM & PRICE	PURCHASER'S NAME/ADD.
8/14/85	Arsenide Compound (7.5 mg As) $3.75	Herman Gibbs' General Store 45 Madison St. Timford, CT
8/30/85	Arsenide Compound (25 mg As) $12.50	Herman Gibbs' General Store 45 Madison St. Timford, CT
9/18/85	Arsenide Compound (50 mg As) $25.00	Herman Gibbs' General Store 45 Madison St. Timford, CT

The final entry was dated 1/19/86, and indicated a purchase of an arsenide compound containing four hundred milligrams of arsenic, for the rather staggering price of two hundred dollars.

"That's quite an extensive vermin problem," Alfred said under his breath. He was rather amazed that Gibbs had been foolish enough to order the stuff directly to his store, rather than have it delivered to his home or some intermediate address. But then, who could believe that any but the most vast and poorly sanitized abode could be plagued by an invasion of rodents so persistent and overwhelming as to require such massive amounts of poison? "Jensen must have had suspicions. But we'll worry about him later."

Alfred's final task was to draft a letter on the other sheet of paper bearing the wafer seal and notary stamp of the Connecticut State Police. He now wound this sheet through his typewriter's platen, thought for a moment, and began to stroke the keys:

February 28, 1886

Connecticut State Police Dept.
1700 Prospect Street
Middletown, Connecticut

Sanford County Sheriff's Dept.
218 Buxton Road
Gunphrey, Connecticut

TO: Officer Samuel Caldwell,
        Sanford County Sheriff

FROM: Officer Richard Alderson,
        Chief Inspector, CSP

Dear Sheriff Caldwell:

I write to inform you that Dr. Alfred Wilson Preston, a fugitive from your jurisdiction, has been taken into our custody here in Middletown. He was located and detained in Frog Hollow upon the basis of an anonymous tip. He is currently gravely ill with pneumonia, but his attending physician at the city jail expects he will make a full recovery within a matter of weeks, whereupon he will be promptly transported to Sanford County to stand trial for the alleged murder of his wife.

All matters pertaining to Dr. Preston's incarceration and medical care are being fully and adequately managed by our department. Thus, you need not reply to this correspondence. Moreover, any public sale of

Dr. Preston's real and personal property authorized by state law may be commenced at the convenience of your county's officials.

Should any unforeseen matter arise which requires your attention, I shall contact you forthwith by letter or telegram. Otherwise, you may expect to receive Dr. Preston into your custody by the end of next month.

Sincerely Yours,

Richard Alderson
Chief Inspector, CSP

P.S. Please do not alert the press regarding this matter, as I fear such exposure might compromise my department's own investigation of Dr. Preston's alleged criminal wrongdoing. Rest assured that I will issue a notice to the newspapers at the appropriate juncture, and that, thereupon, your department shall receive due credit for its tireless efforts in this affair. Much appreciation in advance for your cooperation with this request.

Alfred forged the Inspector's signature, placed the letter inside the second envelope, affixed a stamp to it, and sealed it. He then returned the ledger and the envelope to his briefcase, which he snapped shut and hid beneath his bed.

He would return to Middletown to mail the letter the next day, so that it would bear the proper postmark. And then, finally, he would journey home to Timford.

XII. FURTHER SETBACKS

Alfred awoke at daybreak, feeling energized and robust, ready for his long trip. He dressed in one of several new outfits he had purchased, donned his disguise, and went downstairs. The owner of the boarding house sat in a rocking chair, sipping a mug of coffee.

"I'd like to settle up," Alfred told him. He had informed the owner at the start of the week that he'd likely be leaving within a few days, though wasn't sure exactly when, and asked if he could therefore pay the balance due upon his departure. The owner had happily agreed. "I'm heading back to Mapleton today."

"All right, then." The owner stood and went to the desk, where Alfred joined him and paid what was left of his bill.

"It was a pleasure to have you as a boarder," said the owner.

"It was a pleasure to lodge here. Your accommodations are quite comfortable."

"I appreciate that." Something then flickered in the owner's eyes, a dim recognition, perhaps, or recollection. He furrowed his brow. "Say, it just occurred to me that you look familiar somehow. Not from your boarding here, I don't mean, but from somewhere else. Only I can't quite place where and when it might have been."

Alfred felt his muscles tense. "Hmm. Well, I was once a horse breeder in these parts, and did a stint as a blacksmith in Spring Hill for a few years until I got into the journalism business. Ever been to Spring Hill?"

"Sure," said the owner. "Lots of times. Never commissioned a blacksmith to do any work for me, though. No, I don't think that's it. And I haven't bought a new horse in a long, long time."

Alfred shrugged. "Well, who knows? Perhaps you have me confused with someone else."

The owner contorted his face, scratched his head. "Perhaps so. Well, in any case, have a pleasant day, Mr. Cummings."

Alfred smiled and tipped his hat. "And you, sir."

Alfred stepped outside, into a cool, cloudless day. He looked up at the sky, a perfect azure, frowning severely. He was rattled, disconcerted. It was a damned good thing, he reflected, that he was leaving Danbury within the hour.

He walked past a newsstand, meaning to duck into the diner for a quick breakfast before starting off, and noticed a copy of the *Danbury Register* in one of the racks. The headline blared:

BODY OF MURDER SUSPECT STILL MISSING; FUGITIVE NOW PRESUMED ALIVE AND AT LARGE

Alfred quickly paid the vendor for a copy of the paper, found a nearby alley, and read the article on the front page:

DANBURY, CT – A statewide manhunt shall commence shortly for Alfred Wilson Preston, the affluent mathematician of Timford (pictured on the right) suspected of fatally poisoning his wife. Originally presumed dead, Dr. Preston's body went missing from the Timford Morgue in the early morning hours of February 4th.

Sanford County authorities, in particular Sheriff Caldwell of Timford, now believe that Dr. Preston is alive and at large. "If he were dead," Caldwell told the *Register* during an interview on Wednesday, "his body would have turned up by now. And there's absolutely no reason to suppose that somebody would have, or even *could* have, made off his with body even if he *were* deceased. The notion is patently absurd. The only logical alternative, then, is that he was never dead in the first place but was simply mistaken as so. Which means he's now been on the lam for nearly a month. He could be anywhere by now."

On the same morning that Dr. Preston's remains vanished from the Timford Morgue, a local men's clothing store was burglarized. Investigators discovered footprints and collected several stands of hair from the shop, but noted that without shoes or hair samples to compare them with, such clues are of no value. It is believed that Dr. Preston rifled a false black moustache and matching mutton chops, but that he has since likely dispensed with the disguise and assumed another.

Any persons with knowledge of Dr. Preston's whereabouts, or who believe they may have seen him, are ordered under penalty of law to report such information directly and without delay to the Sanford County Sheriff's Department.

Furious, Alfred ripped the paper to shreds and disposed of them in a trash barrel. He told himself to be calm, reminded himself that he had dated the letter four days in advance, lest just such a contingency arise. But his anger and disquiet were nonetheless difficult to subdue, and he waited a moment before emerging from the alley.

He would have to take breakfast in another town en route to Middletown, a small town where newspapers carrying similar articles were unlikely to be circulated. And he would have to delay his arrival in the city by at least three days. That would mean lodging in various inns for three nights. He was already running low on money and another three days of exposure would vastly increase his risk of being recognized. But what choice had he?

Moving quickly, cursing under his breath, he unhitched Lucy from a post outside the boarding house, mounted her, and rode off toward Middletown.

He arrived in Middletown at quarter of noon three days later. He found the nearest post office box and deposited the letter to Caldwell. He then hurriedly turned and rode Lucy at a steady gallop until he was clear of the city, darting over the nearest hill and through a dense wood, finally letting the mare relax her stride.

After traveling another five or six miles, he pulled on the reins and brought her to a stop. He dismounted her, hitched her to a tree, and sat down on a rock for a moment, needing to think. He rested his elbows on his knees and his chin on his hands, staring down at the ground as he contemplated his plight. What if another newspaper article about him appeared after Caldwell received the letter? What if all the gates around his estate were locked and guarded, his servants having been evicted? What if he couldn't procure the sort of evidence against Caldwell that he hoped to? And what if, even if he did, nobody from the State Police showed on the day of the auction?

A sinister rattle intruded upon his thoughts and he looked up suddenly, saw a timber rattlesnake coiled up about six feet from the rock. That such a creature should be roaming the land in weather so cold was an extreme aberration. A wave of vicious déjà vu crashed over him as Lucy began to whinny volubly and reared up on her haunches. He squelched the panic that blossomed in his chest and kept perfectly still, forcing himself to think clearly.

The constable's gun, presumably loaded, was in the pommel bag tied to Lucy's saddle. Lucy herself was in a terrible fright, and there was no way he could calm her long enough to unhitch and mount her. But if he could just get into the saddlebag and retrieve the gun, he could shoot the snake dead.

He rose, very slowly, and took small, gingerly steps toward the mare. She was kicking and fussing, whipping her head from side to side. He spoke to her in a soft voice, repeating her name as he struggled to still her sufficiently to open the saddlebag and remove the revolver. Just as he was sliding it out, she turned to bite him, and he evaded her teeth by perhaps half a second.

He looked back at the snake. It remained coiled in a tight ball, its forked tongue flicking in and out at lightning-fast speed. Alfred had fired a few rifles in his day, but never a handgun. He lifted it now to chest-level, cocked the hammer, and aimed directly for the serpent's head. The first shot missed completely, sending up a huge cloud of dust and causing Lucy to thrash so violently that she nearly snapped the hitching rope in half. Alfred recovered from the recoil, which had knocked him back about three feet, and cocked the gun again. He steadied his hands and took a second shot.

The snake's head split in two, blood splattering the ground across a radius of a dozen yards. Swatches of skin and shattered fragments of jawbone and jagged remnants of fangs exploded into the air, alighting in and between the wide rivers of blood. The report from the gun echoed deafeningly against the trees, making his ears ring like church bells. Lucy continued to flail and snort for another minute or two and then at last began to settle down.

Alfred let out a long, shivery breath. Trembling a little, he unhitched his mare from the tree, climbed atop her, and squeezed his legs gently against her sides. At first she simply stood there, frozen with lingering fear, and then, eventually, got moving.

He rode until sunset, whereupon he checked into a three-room inn in Tip's Creek, a tiny hamlet about thirty-six miles due east of Timford. He stayed there for three nights, wanting to ensure that Caldwell would have received the letter from Alderson before returning to Timford.

Alfred, well aware that he would need a new and far more elaborate disguise than either of his previous two, had patronized another pharmacy and a men's shop between Danbury and Middletown. From the pharmacy he had purchased a jar of makeup, a six-ounce canister of flesh-colored putty, a small bottle of beeswax, a jar of petroleum jelly, a pouch of nightshade, and an eye-shadow brush. Before the mirror over the dresser, Alfred now sat and applied each item carefully: the makeup to his cheekbones to create the impression of wrinkles; a few gobs of the putty to reshape his nose; crusts of beeswax around his lips; daubs of the petroleum jelly to his forehead to create a sickly sheen; and finally, with the brush, the red nightshade to his eyelids, arousing in them a fierce burning sensation. He kept the wig but discarded the beard.

He leaned forward and appraised his new appearance. He looked like a terribly old, ailing man on the verge of death, perhaps infected with some virulent strain of disease. He smiled faintly, felt the beeswax stretch on his lips, and rose from the wing char. He gathered his last two purchases (these from the men's shop), a gnarled wooden cane with a brass knob and a pair of iron-framed, double-hinged spectacles with clear oval lenses, and then retrieved his briefcase from under his bed. He donned the spectacles, took up the cane in his right hand, and carried the briefcase in his left.

It was about quarter of three in the morning. Alfred crept downstairs, peeked around the corner, saw the front desk abandoned, and made haste for the door.

Lucy was asleep. He woke her with a gentle shake, unhitched her, mounted her, and started off for Timford.

XIII. RETURNING HOME

He rode in utter darkness to his estate. As he approached the front gates, he saw that none of the lamps was lit and that the manor itself was pitch-black, apparently abandoned. He had expected and feared as much.

He yanked on Lucy's reins and brought her to a stop, dismounted her, and went up to the gates. Straining his eyes, he could make out in the bright moonlight a big padlock securing the gates together and, above it, attached with heavy bolts, a sign which read: "THIS PROPERTY SEIZED BY THE SANFORD COUNTY SHERIFF'S DEPARTMENT. TRESPASSERS WILL BE PROSECUTED TO THE FULLEST EXTENT OF THE LAW!"

Alfred looked around, terrified of being spotted even at this obscenely early hour. He thought about trying to pick or smash the lock, and then thought of a better idea. He hopped onto Lucy and guided her around to the back of the estate, through wilted flowerbeds and frost-covered ornamental shrubs, over rocks and frozen grass. When they reached the backside of the estate, he dismounted her again and hitched her to the tall, wrought-iron fence which girdled the grounds. There was a low point in the fence, an architectural oddity to which Alfred had paid little mind during his residence in the home, but which he'd remembered well enough to contrive a means inside.

He got on Lucy and told her to hold steady for a moment, then grabbed one of the rails and slowly erected himself, until he was balancing himself on her saddle. She fussed a bit but held mostly still. He stepped cautiously onto the low bar in the dip in the fence, using the higher rails for support, and then jumped the six feet or so to the ground on the other side.

He landed squarely on his feet, staggered to the left, and then righted himself. The tendons in his ankles had flared for a moment, causing him slight pain, but he hadn't sprained anything, as he'd feared he might. He turned and went to the fence and slid his arm through two of the rails, patting Lucy on her hindquarters. "Thanks, girl," he said. "Back in a flash."

He used a rock to the break the window in the back door, unlatched the lock, and let himself in. He stumbled about until he'd found his way into the parlor, rustled up some candles from a drawer in the Victorian hutch, and used a match from the book in his pocket to light one. He then went to the mantelpiece over the fireplace, pulled down a candelabra, and inserted the lit candle into one of the arms. After lighting and inserting the other two candles, he made his way into the kitchen.

He went directly to the waste bin, opened it, and was knocked back by the stench of rotting food. Evidently Thomas had heeded his last instruction in the telegram. Alfred set the candelabra down on the island counter, pinched his nose, and began rifling through the garbage. Eventually he came up with it: the empty bag of flour he'd bought from Herman Gibbs's general store a month ago to the day. He peeled off some fruit skins and plum seeds which had encrusted themselves to the bag, dusted it off, tied its strings around his belt, and retrieved the candelabra from the counter.

Next he climbed the stairs to his bedroom, where awful images of Claudia and Beatrice standing over Julia's withered, perished body crowded his mind. He drove them out by sheer will, went to his bureau, and set the candelabra on top of it. He opened the top drawer, removed a false bottom, and scooped together a pile of fifty-dollar bills, which he then stuffed into his coat pocket. He closed the drawer and picked up the candelabra.

He was halfway across the room when he stopped suddenly in his tracks. Because he could not help himself, he cast an uneasy glance at the bed in which Julia had died, *their* bed, now bereft of its sheets and coverlet. He imagined her now, not sick, not dying, but instead vigorous and hardy, whistling a melody while arranging flowers on the bedstand, preparing to paint a mural or play her violin in the sunroom. The image made his heart ache unbearably, stirred a longing for her presence, her touch so intense that he nearly fell to his knees.

And then, with tears in his eyes, he thought: *All of this, everything you've done, will be meaningless if you fall apart now. All your tedious and numberless labors will have been in vain. You must avenge her death, that those who took her from you might face the punishment they deserve, and that you might find peace, be free to mourn her passing and, perhaps someday, put her cherished memory to rest.*

These thoughts invigorated Alfred anew, revived at once his weary but unwavering resolve. He averted his eyes from the bed and forced himself to get moving. He carried the candelabra into the hallway, gently closing the bedroom door behind him.

He went downstairs to his study, went to his desk, and opened the bottom drawer, where he kept correspondence, tax records, business receipts, and the like. He sifted through the documents until, much to his surprise, he came upon them: the last twelve receipts from Gibbs's store, narrow egg-shell white slips of ruled paper on which his name, all his purchases, and their prices had been sloppily but legibly notated. He dug out, as well, a document prepared by his personal accountant last autumn which listed the values of all his assets, both individually and taken together.

Evidently Caldwell and his boys were too preoccupied with finding me to obtain a search warrant. That, or they were simply too incompetent to find things they surely would have otherwise seized.

He folded the papers into quarters and slipped them into the breast pocket of his coat, carried the candelabra to the back foyer, set it on a pedestal, and blew out the candles.

Letting himself out the back door, he made his way across the lawn, the soles of his boots crunching over the frost. He wrapped his scarf tighter around his neck as a strong gust of wind rippled the hair on his wig. He saw Lucy nodding off by the fence, felt a pang of guilt for all the endless and extensive traveling to which he'd subjected her, particularly in such harsh weather.

There was a willow tree a few feet from the dip in the fence, and he shimmied up it now like a cat, hoisting himself from branch to branch until he was high enough to pass himself down along one of the stouter branches, which drooped under his weight as he crossed it fist by fist, like an amateur trapeze artist turned upside-down. Eventually he was low enough to plant his feet on the bar and grip the two rails on either side. Wobbling a bit, he then lowered himself onto Lucy's back, sidesaddle, and hopped onto the ground.

After checking to make sure he still had everything he'd come for, he unhitched his mare, mounted her astride, and took off through the frigid night air, bound for the courthouse in Gunphrey.

The streets were empty, though the moon now hung low in the sky and dawn was not far off. Alfred hitched Lucy to a post at the foot of the courthouse steps and climbed them, noticing for the first time that the pain in his right shoulder had largely abated.

He went to the big, stately double doors and saw the sign he knew he would, affixed to the right-hand door with some sort of adhesive. The words were dimly visible in the moonlight:

PRESTON ESTATE TO BE
AUCTIONED
ON THESE PREMISES
FRIDAY, MARCH 8TH, 1886 AT
NOON;
SEALED BIDS ACCEPTED
UNTIL 6 P.M. ON MARCH 7TH AT
COUNTY CLERK'S OFFICE

March 8th, Alfred thought. *Five days from now.*

He turned, looked both ways, and saw a gentleman in a top hat and long black coat walking along the street, toward the courthouse. He was tall and slender, carried an ivory-capped scrimshaw cane in his right hand.

Alfred quickly descended the steps of the courthouse, trying to remain hidden in the shadows, but the man spotted him the moment he reached the street.

"Hello, there!" he called out.

"Good morning," Alfred said, feigning a Swiss accent. He gave a polite wave.

The man waved back and came closer, until he was just a few feet away. His long, slender face was ashen in the moonlight, a dull yellow resembling mild jaundice. "Up early today, are we?"

"No earlier than you," Alfred said with a wink. "I suffer bouts of insomnia, I'm afraid. I find that taking brief strolls sometimes cures them."

"Ah," said the man. "I've had a rather sleepless night myself. My sister Mildred's come down with tuberculosis. The doctors fear she won't make it."

"I'm terribly sorry to hear that," Alfred said, carefully minding his accent. He deliberately drooped his shoulders and lilted to one side. "I believe I may be growing ill myself. I've had dizzy spells of late, and terrible weakness in my limbs. I might do well to see a doctor of my own."

"Yes," said the fellow in the top hat, "you *don't* look terribly well, if I may say so."

Alfred nodded feebly. "If you'll excuse me, I'm rather tired now. I'd best get home and try to sleep."

"Of course."

Alfred turned toward Lucy, inwardly sighing with relief.

"Say," said the man, "I noticed you were perusing the sign on the courthouse door. Do you plan to bid on the Preston estate, if I may ask?"

Alfred turned back slowly, as if in pain, and smiled wanly. "The thought had crossed my mind, yes. If I'm well enough to attend the auction, that is."

The gentleman smiled back, revealing brown, crooked teeth, and raised his cane to waist-level, wielding it like a lance. "We're sworn enemies, then, it would seem. I plan to put in a bid myself. And I'm quite well-to-do."

"Well," Alfred said, "I wish you the best of luck, sir. Excuse me."

The man bade him farewell and continued on his way. Alfred waited until he was out of sight, unhitched Lucy, and rode off as fast as she would carry him.

XIV. ANOTHER LETTER

Alfred found an inn in another remote hamlet about twenty miles south of Timford. He checked in at dawn under the name of Walter Givens. The innkeeper asked if he was feeling all right.

"Just a touch of the flu," he said, now affecting a British accent. "But the doctor assures me I'm no longer contagious."

"Best not be," said the innkeeper, a hulking man with dark, scraggly stubble and an odd film over one eye, obscured by the dusty lens of an ill-fitting monocle. "Don't need my other lodgers gettin' sick."

"I won't have any contact with them, sir. I won't be leaving my room much, and intend to depart within a few days."

The innkeeper nodded reluctantly, took Alfred's money, made change, and handed him a key. "Enjoy your stay," he said.

Alfred had abandoned his typewriter at the boarding house in Danbury, as it had been far too unwieldy to transport by horseback, but he had kept hold of his fountain pen. He had replaced the red ink with black, and now sat hunched over a decrepit oak table in the corner of his room, drafting a letter to Richard Alderson, Chief Inspector of the Connecticut State Police. He had written the date and headings, and now began work on the body of the epistle:

Dear Inspector Alderson,

I am writing regarding a most sensitive and urgent matter. I have come into possession of physical evidence that Samuel Caldwell, the Sheriff of Sanford County, as well as Herman Gibbs, sole owner and proprietor of Timford's general store, conspired to cause the death of Julia Preston, wife of Dr. Alfred W. Preston, her alleged murderer. This evidence is concrete and conclusive, but I am afraid that I am unable to disclose its nature in this letter, lest it be somehow intercepted and retribution be exacted upon me. I have kept the evidence in question carefully concealed since I obtained it, and will not unveil it save in the presence of a State Police officer.

The auction of Dr. Preston's estate is set for noon on March 8th, at which time and place Sheriff Caldwell shall be present. This seems to me the most prudent and appropriate occasion upon which to reveal the aforesaid proof of his and Mr.

Gibbs's criminal conduct. I am therefore requesting that one or more officers from your department be dispatched to the Sanford County Courthouse on the day and at the time of the auction, that Sheriff Caldwell might thereupon be taken into custody. I furthermore have reason to believe that Mr. Gibbs will be present, as well.

Please be advised that I do not know Dr. Preston or have any knowledge of his whereabouts. I simply feel, given the evidence I have uncovered, that it is both my moral duty and legal obligation to vindicate him in the matter of this terrible crime, as well as to insure that Sheriff Caldwell and Mr. Gibbs are brought to justice for their malfeasance.

Sir, I cannot overstate the significance and solidity of the evidence to which I refer, nor how profoundly important it is that at least one officer from your department be present at the auction to consider this evidence and act accordingly. I implore you to heed my exhortation, that the

abominable transgression at hand not go
unpunished, nor the two men culpable for it be
afforded an opportunity to escape.

I write this letter with the utmost sincerity and
truthfulness. Again, please take heed of what I
have conveyed, that this longstanding matter
might be finally and fairly resolved.

With Great Earnestness,

Walter Givens

He read over the letter and, satisfied with it,
sealed it in a long brown envelope, which he addressed
to Alderson. He then placed it in his briefcase, in whose
inner pocket he had stashed the ledger, bills of sale, and
receipts from Gibbs's store. As had become his custom,
he hid the briefcase under his bed.

Remote and sparsely populated as the village
was, there was fortunately located a post office at the
western end of its single dirt road. Alfred would mail

the letter from there later in the day, paying for express delivery. The letter would reach Alderson's desk by the 5th or 6th, giving the inspector plenty of time to deploy an officer or two to the auction. Provided, of course, that he took Alfred's admonition seriously.

And if, in the meantime, Alfred couldn't obtain the manner of evidence he hoped to, the whole endeavor would have been for naught. Mere embarrassment would be the least of his worries. He would be collared on the spot, and Caldwell and Gibbs would go free, the latter left to snatch up Alfred's estate while Alfred himself rotted in a prison cell for the rest of his life – or else, as Caldwell had cheerfully noted, marched up to the gallows.

The ledger would be enough to put Gibbs away, he told himself. *Or at least subject him to an intensive investigation.*

But deep down he knew better. Gibbs might have a hard time accounting for why he'd order enough arsenic to kill a small elephant (even *qua* merchant), much less a hundred-and-twenty-pound woman, but merely that he *had* would hardly suffice to support a charge of homicide in any degree. Ultimately he would concoct some story just plausible enough to explain away his anomalous purchases, walk away a free man, and acquire Alfred's estate for perhaps one-third its market value.

Sighing, Alfred undressed and climbed into bed.

He would need to find the missing link – and soon.

XV. A RISKY ENDEAVOR

He was in a dilemma. On the one hand, he couldn't afford to wait until the night before the auction to hunt down the evidence he sought; it was anybody's guess how long it might take him to unearth it, assuming he ever could - and that it was somewhere to be unearthed in the first place. On the other hand, if he went searching and found it too soon, and it was then discovered missing before the day of the auction, his whole enterprise would be foiled.

Moreover, where in the hell ought he look first? And how many failed attempts could he afford before he was caught? He wasn't even certain what it was he meant to look *for*, much less where it might be. All he knew, or strongly suspected, was that there was, *somewhere*, some manner of evidence, most likely a paper trail of sorts, linking both Caldwell and Gibbs to Julia's death. But where was it most plausibly to be located, and how might he get to it?

Start with the facts, then, he thought now, sitting on the edge of his bed. *Start with what you know to be the case, and work from there. You know, first of all, that Gibbs ordered lethal quantities of arsenic from Jensen's pharmacy. You know, secondly, that Gibbs bags his own flour and thus could have easily added increasing amounts of the poison to the sacks of flour he sold you, well aware that you yourself would never consume anything made with it. You know, thirdly, that the county is authorized to auction your estate and seize your assets in the event of your incarceration for a capital crime. You know, fourthly, that Caldwell will either be tasked with organizing and administering the auction or else request the role, and so could rig it in such a way as to guarantee that Gibbs's is the highest bid.*

But exactly how *could* Caldwell guarantee that Gibbs's would be the highest bid? What if some affluent businessman, such as Alfred had encountered on the street in Gunphrey, came along and offered a figure close to the estate's market value? The only way Caldwell could guarantee that Gibbs's would be the highest bid, then, would be to ensure somehow that Gibbs *himself* could pay market value. But if Gibbs were forced to bid market value, or even close to it, then what would either man have stood to gain from the collusion?

Nothing. Precisely nothing. Unless, of course…

Unless the money Gibbs used to purchase the estate were money that was never his in the first place, money that he wouldn't be spending out of his or Caldwell's own pocket (or both). Money, for example, that never made it to the agency to which, if Alfred were in fact incarcerated, it would lawfully belong: the Sanford County Treasury.

Your liquid assets alone vastly exceed the market value of your estate. Add to those the total value of your various stocks and bonds and sundry other holdings and the total would likely top three million dollars. All of those assets now belong to the county. All of them, by now, would have been placed in an escrow account, a trust, held by the County Treasury and managed, most likely, by Timford's town bank. And Caldwell, in all probability, would have been the one charged with seizing the assets. Thus, all Caldwell would have to have done was to squirrel away a portion of my assets into a separate account, under Gibbs's name, and then turn over the remainder to the county. Would the Treasurer or the Assessor have any reason to doubt the Sheriff's integrity, to question the total value of the assets seized? Or any inclination to investigate the true worth of those assets? Surely not. Thus, Gibbs would need merely to write a check against the secret account to finance the purchase of the estate. The check would be deposited into the County Treasury, all the numbers would add up in the ledger, and…

"And Gibbs would be free to sell the estate on the free market, reaping the entire ill-begotten sum as pure profit, on top of whatever might remain in the newly opened account. Profit, of course, to be split with Caldwell. Most likely fifty-fifty, but maybe more to Gibbs on account of his greater role and thus greater risk in the collaboration."

His mind racing now, Alfred began pacing around the room, gnawing on his thumbnail. Would either fellow be so reckless as to leave sitting about some record of their ruse? Deposit slips, bank receipts, a list of the hidden assets? Surely not. Surely one or the other would have set any such documentation aflame, consigning it to oblivion. On the other hand, surely Caldwell wouldn't have been stupid enough to forge the county assessor's signature on the back of a bank draft and endorse it over to Gibbs. The only safe way of getting the hidden assets into a secret account would have been to withdraw *cash*, hand it over to Gibbs, and let Gibbs deposit it, perhaps under the pretense that he'd inherited a fortune from a rich uncle or cashed in all his oil or railroad stocks - harvested a windfall of *some* origin, in other words.

Alfred sat back down on the bed, his mind no longer racing but now spinning. The narrative made perfect sense, was eminently plausible, and, he knew in his gut, was absolutely *true*. But still, still, there remained the problem of *proof.*

And then something occurred to him: *Gibbs and Caldwell have known each other since they were boys, yes, but with a scheme of this size and complexity, a crime of this magnitude, trusting one's co-conspirator to honor his end of the bargain would be no easy business. What assurance would Caldwell have that Gibbs wouldn't bolt with the whole sum and steal off to Mexico or Venezuela or any damned place? His word alone? Somehow that wouldn't seem likely to satisfy a man like Samuel Caldwell. Trust has never been one of his most salient qualities.*

A contract, then. A contract to be enforced in the unlikely event that Gibbs attempted to renege on the deal. A contract stipulating, perhaps, that Caldwell was entitled to some percentage of the proceeds from the sale of Alfred's estate in exchange for services rendered, goods supplied, or money loaned. Would the enforcement of such a contract raise eyebrows? Perhaps. But most likely not, so long as the original fraudulent transaction had been successfully disguised and the conspiracy itself never revealed. And if Gibbs made a run for it just the same, so that the contract couldn't be enforced at all? Caldwell would have him lassoed before he could make it as far as New York, charge him with any crime he liked.

So where, then, might such a contract be kept, and by whom? Somewhere in safe hiding, of course, and by the party with an interest in it, the party that would seek to enforce it if necessary. Sheriff Caldwell, in other words.

And what safer place to hide such a document, Alfred asked himself now, than in the fellow's very own house?

*   *   *

The waiting was torturous. He left the inn only twice, once to purchase a lantern, a chisel, a pry bar, and enough food to last him for the remaining three days, and once to perform a bit of covert scouting. He went over his plan again and again, as much as it could be *called* a plan, resenting each time the rather considerable element of imprecision. Anything could go wrong at any step of the way, and if it did, as with every previous risk he had taken, the whole design would come crashing down upon him, all his arduous trials rendered worthless, and with disastrous consequences.

So yes, the risk was grave, indeed, monumental. The biggest yet by far. But as so often before, it seemed there was no alternative. It would have to be done. And tonight would be his final opportunity to do it.

He took a deep breath and went to the dresser, sat before the mirror, painstakingly re-applied his disguise. (Not, of course, that a disguise would do him much good if he were caught during *this* particular adventure, but he didn't want to take the extra risk of being spotted en route to or from Caldwell's house.) He put the brush down, sealed the bottle of beeswax (nearly empty now), and then threw all the cosmetic items into the waste bin. By the time they were found, it would all be over – one way or another.

Now he packed the chisel and pry bar into one of his satchels and slung it over his left shoulder, checked to make sure there was a book of matches in his coat pocket. He took up his lantern, not yet lit, and crept downstairs. He gave a nod to the innkeeper (half-asleep in his cottage pine chair), and went outside.

Lucy, his faithful sidekick, was awake and alert, almost as if she'd been expecting him.

He hitched her to a streetlamp about a quarter-mile from Caldwell's house, which as luck had it was set out somewhat in the country. There would be no neighbors to disturb, no meddlesome passers-by. He took the satchel from the saddlebag, draped it over his shoulder, and looked around. All was quiet.

He gave Lucy a little pat below her neck and told her he'd be back soon. He could only pray it was the truth. Turning up the collar of his coat against the biting wind, toting the lantern in his right hand, he started off on the longish walk to Sheriff Caldwell's residence, a two-story red-brick with four windows on the ground floor. Alfred hadn't dared get close enough to be sure of it, but from what he *had* been able to glean, they had at least appeared to be of the sash variety. The strap of his satchel was already beginning to dig into the flesh of his left shoulder from the weight of the pry bar. He would have to switch it back and forth between his shoulders until he arrived, putting less burden on the right.

A light snow began to fall, glistening under the light of another near-full, luminescent moon. Moist flakes alighted and melted on Alfred's crimson cheeks. Ten minutes into the walk, he had started to sweat rather profusely, and the weight of the satchel had become almost intolerable. He simply carried it now by the strap with his left hand, the lantern in his other, trudging up the dirt trail that led to the Sheriff's dwelling.

Once within fifty feet of it, he was careful to keep hidden in the shadows, out of the moonlight. He skulked a bit closer to the house, a bit closer yet, and then dropped to all fours. He hooked the satchel around one of his feet and dragged it behind him (on the fresh coat of snow it made little noise) as he scrabbled toward one of the windows, the window he believed led into Caldwell's study.

For all you know it's his bedroom. For all you know he sleeps on the ground floor.

But he couldn't listen to such thoughts right now. He had already resolved to do what he was about to, and that was that, the consequences be damned.

He reached the window, finally, and leaned back against the brick wall, softly panting. He shook the satchel loose and then just sat there for a moment, catching his breath and steeling himself for what came next. Then he reached down for the satchel, unbuckled its clasps, and removed the chisel.

He started at a noise, nearly dropping the blasted chisel, and then relaxed as he realized it was just a small animal, probably a possum, scuttering through the snow. His nerves were live wires. He took a deep breath, waited for his heart to slow, reminding himself that staying collected was half the job. He would need a clear head and steady hands to see this venture through, and as he was, he had neither.

So he waited a few moments more. There was, after all, no great hurry. He had arrived late enough that the Sheriff was almost certainly asleep, but plenty early enough to afford himself the luxury of being deliberate and methodical. Not, of course, that any dilly-dallying would do. He would spend not a minute longer on these premises than was absolutely necessary to accomplish his goal.

And so, after a few more minutes of simply breathing slowly and letting his jitters wane, he rose to his knees, lit the lantern, turned, and shone it through the window. He saw a desk, several bookcases, a floor globe, and what appeared to be a mahogany drafting table. The room was Caldwell's study, after all.

Alfred looked about again, saw nothing but trees and falling snow, extinguished the lantern and picked up the chisel.

Carefully, he thought. *Slowly. Patiently.*

He forced the blade of the chisel between the sash and the sill and began to wiggle it, his gloved fingers trembling only slightly.

After five minutes of cautious, quiet maneuvering, he finally managed to get the sash up just high enough with the chisel to squeeze in the curved end of the pry bar. Now he dropped the chisel and pressed down, ever so gently, on the flat handle of the pry. He had to be exceedingly careful not to break the glass. He applied an ounce more pressure, then another ounce, and then, *voila!* The lock at the top of the sash snapped almost soundlessly, simply fissuring along its middle.

Alfred shivered with relief, then quickly replaced the tools into his satchel and slid the window open just wide enough so that he could climb through, lantern in hand. There were fortunately no obstructions in his path, and he landed softly on what felt like a thick pile rug. The room was pitch-black, save for the sliver of moonlight that leaked through the dusty window. He closed the window quickly but quietly, to shut out the draft, and then bent down to relight his lantern.

It cast a harsh yellow glare upon the objects in the arc of its light. The pile rug on which he stood appeared to be Egyptian, with a most intricate and exquisite pattern woven into it, with all the familiar flowers, palmettes, lotuses, and arabesques. The walls were covered with wallpaper bearing similarly complex designs, the floor itself constructed of heart pine. There was a bookcase behind the desk and two against the walls on either side of it. The door on the other side of the study was firmly closed.

He went first to the drafting table, on which there lay a sketch of a western-style ranch house of elaborate design and considerable proportions. It was surrounded by a vast lawn and accompanying pasture, with horse stables and a cow pen off in the distance. The depiction was very well rendered, which was hardly surprising in light of Caldwell's previous experience as an architect. Descrying in the sketch no significance to the culprits' scheme, or any relevance to the task at hand, Alfred now turned from the drafting table and moved the lantern to and fro, in vague circles, as if blindly casting a fishing line in the hopes of catching a nibble.

And then he did: there was something odd about the bookcase behind the desk (whose drawers he would investigate momentarily); it seemed to jut out slightly from the wall rather than simply stand against it, rather as if it were *hinged* to it.

He carried the lantern over to the bookcase, set it down noiselessly on the floor, and reached for the right side panel. He ran his hand along its smooth oak surface, his heart beating faster now, and then gripped it and gave it a small tug toward his body. It moved effortlessly, and when he opened it wider, he saw a recess in the wall behind it.

And, mounted in the recess, a combination wall safe.

Alfred knew by the brand and style of the safe that the combination would consist of six numbers. But how in the hell was he supposed to deduce what those numbers might *be*?

Think. You've plenty of time. You haven't made so much as a peep thus far, and there's been no stirring from upstairs. So just clear your mind and think. What set of numbers might one use as a combination to his safe? It would be a set easy for him to remember but difficult for anyone save perhaps those who knew him, and whom he trusted, to guess.

On the other hand, it might be entirely random, jotted down somewhere on a slip of paper or the inside of a journal kept securely tucked away.

A thought flashed through his mind then, a recollection of an encounter with Caldwell at Gibbs's store the year before. The second week of last April, it had been. It would have been a Wednesday, as Alfred had always gone shopping on Wednesday afternoons. He could hear Herman's voice in his head, talking to Caldwell: *I understand you've got a birthday coming up, old pal. This Saturday, isn't it?* Caldwell had grinned good-naturedly and conceded the fact, then noted with a playful grimace that he was turning forty-five.

Today is Friday, March 8th, Alfred thought. That means April 8th will be a Monday, and thus April 10th a Wednesday. If April 10th of this year will be a Wednesday, then April 10th of last year would have been a Tuesday. So I was at the store on April 11th. Saturday would have been the 14th. So Caldwell would have turned forty-five on April 14th, 1885. Which makes his birthday April 14th, 1840.

0-6-1-4-4-0.

Could it really be that simple? It seemed impossible, but it was worth a try. Alfred raised the lantern to eye-level, spun the dial to the zero, around to the six, back to the one, around again to the five, back to the four, and finally back again to the zero. He listened for a *click* and heard nothing. He pulled on the handle but the door didn't budge at all.

Goddammit! You fool! Caldwell may not be Newton, but neither is he a total dolt. Think, damn you! He could wake at any moment.

A fresh panic taking hold of him now, Alfred turned around and looked at the desk, looked at the three drawers on its left-hand side and the narrower drawer above the kneehole. He picked up the lantern and tip-toed over to the desk, setting the lantern on its mostly bare surface. He tried the drawer above the kneehole and found it locked. He tried next the top drawer in the set of three. It opened easily, and Alfred shone the lantern upon its contents: pens, pencils, blank note cards, some push-pins, and a letter-opener. He dug deeper, sifting through the jumble of stationery and whatnot with a kind of frenzied determination, though remained careful to be quiet. Eventually satisfied that there was nothing of interest in the drawer, he closed it and tried the second one down.

This one contained a stack of cardboard folders and, beneath them, a leather-bound notebook. He removed this latter from the drawer and opened it upon the desk. The first page was filled mostly with doodles and illegible scribbles, an address written in the center with a box drawn around it. It was an address in Pine Haven which meant nothing to Alfred. He turned to the next page and saw what appeared to be hastily scrawled case notes and personal reflections on the suspects in question. He flipped to the next page and found more of the same, along with another meaningless address and a reminder to put in a request with the County Commissioner for more mail baskets and rubber erasers. Getting flustered, Alfred riffled through the remaining pages, saw nothing of import, and was about to put the notebook back into the drawer when something came loose from a notch on the back cover and fluttered to the floor.

It was a square of thin yellow cardboard. Alfred bent and picked it up, held it up to the lantern. Written across it in India ink, with rather meticulous care, were six numbers separated by dashes: "8 – 11 – 16 – 5 – 4- 18."

Ah ha! Alfred could barely contain a cry of joy, but cautioned himself that the numbers might hold an altogether different significance, or serve simply as a red herring to would-be thieves.

There was, of course, but one way to find out. He replaced the card in the notch in the notebook, having committed the sequence of numbers to memory, and then placed the notebook itself back in the drawer. He closed the drawer and picked up the lantern and carried it back to the safe. Holding the lantern at chest-level, he spun the dial back to zero, then rotated it to the designated numbers in the order written. As he aligned the "18" with the notch line on the rim around the dial, he heard the tumbler fall into place and the lock spring free. Success!

Glancing nervously over his shoulder, Alfred now eased the safe-door open and peered inside. What he found astonished him, and he could hardly stifle a gasp.

He grabbed up the documents as quickly as he could, closed the safe-door (rather too loudly in his excitement), and spun the dial. Just as he was backing out of the recess behind the bookcase, there came a creaking of floorboards directly above him. There came footsteps from upstairs.

Oh, Christ. Please, no, not now. Not when I'm this close!

He's up, Alfred. He's awake. You're done for.

Sweat rolling off his brow like rainwater, he stuffed the papers into the breast pocket of his coat, crumpling them in his haste, and immediately extinguished the lantern.

Deep Cold

"Who's there?" Caldwell cried from the top of the stairs. His voice was gruff and sleepy. "Is someone there?"

Alfred side-stepped back into the recess, pulled the bookcase closed as quietly as he could, and then simply stood there, frozen with fear. He tried not to twitch so much as a finger, to breathe in perfect silence. He could feel his heartbeat thudding in his temples.

He waited and listened, his anxiety almost unbearable. He wanted to scream, to throw open the bookcase and sprint to the window, dive through it and make a mad dash for Lucy. But all he could do was stand there like a statue, awaiting his fate. He bit his bottom lip hard enough to draw blood.

Did I put the notebook back in the drawer and close it? Did I disturb anything else? He couldn't remember. His mind was a total fog. *Where's the yellow card with the combination on it? Did I replace it in the notebook? And what if Caldwell comes into the study? What if I forgot to –*

More footsteps now, descending the stairs. "I said who goes there?" Caldwell repeated. He was perhaps halfway down the staircase now. "I'll shoot you square between the eyes, whoever you are."

Alfred tried to swallow but couldn't. The lantern was quivering in his hands. His whole body was now soaked with sweat.

Caldwell took another few steps down the stairs, coughing and grunting. He was nearly in the foyer now. "Is that you, Bernadine?"

Bernadine? Who the hell is Bernadine? Caldwell isn't married.

"Dammit, cat, if you're going through the garbage again, I swear I'll put your furry butt out for good."

Oh, thank God. A cat. Caldwell has a cat. Alfred let out a tiny sigh, his heart gradually slowing.

"Bernadine? Ah, there you are. You gave me one hell of a fright. What on earth was all that ruckus about, anyhow? Did you knock something over?"

He heard a cat meow, and then saw a flash of candlelight as Caldwell opened the door to the study. Bernadine raced inside and, by the sound of it, jumped onto the desk chair. She was purring loudly now, and Alfred imagined her tail switching against the drawer from which he'd plucked the notebook.

No, he thought. *No, please.*

"Have you been jumping on my damn desk again? I've told you to keep outta here a hundred times, ya damned pest!"

The cat let out another, far shriller meow and leapt off the chair as Caldwell swatted her with his hand. The candlelight flickered ominously on the narrow band of wall that Alfred could glimpse through the crack in the bookcase. Caldwell turned, hesitated for a moment, and then took a single step toward it, toward the bookcase behind which Alfred stood hiding and trembling. For a moment there prevailed an excruciatingly pregnant silence, permeating the room like a noxious gas.

Alfred was certain, now, that he'd left behind some noticeable trace of his forced entry. A diminutive yet detectable puddle of water on the rug, perhaps, from the snow which had melted on the soles of his boots. Or a drawer not fully closed. Or, worse yet, the notebook lying in plain view upon the desk. And could Caldwell hear him breathing, hear the minute sound of his feet tapping against the floor, his knees' knocking ever so slightly together? Could he hear the tiny, metallic rattle of the lantern? Could he hear, somehow, Alfred's racing heart?

"Damned cat," Caldwell muttered, then turned and left the study, closing the door behind him.

Alfred now heard footsteps ascending the stairs, a door closing in the hallway overhead.

And then, once more, perfect silence.

XVI. EXAMINING THE PROOF

Alfred got back to the inn about an hour before sunup. Cold and exhausted, he wanted only to curl up in bed and go to sleep. But he knew slumber would be impossible, as well as imprudent (he could not afford to sleep past eleven). Though exceedingly weary, he was far too keyed-up, his mind much too awake and alert, to permit even a brief doze.

Besides, he had the documents to examine, documents at which he had scarcely glanced, and only under enormous emotional strain and the dimmest of light. Now, with his lantern at full glow and two candelabras lit, he took the papers from his satchel and laid them out on the craggy oak table in the corner of his room. He looked first at one of the Certificate of Stock Cash-Out Receipts, studying it intently:

CERTIFICATE OF STOCK
CASH-OUT RECEIPT

NAME OF STOCKHOLDER: Dr. Alfred W. Preston

COMPANY: Brown & Bros. Bank

NO. OF SHARES: 782

VALUE PER SHARE: $38.29

TOTAL VALUE OF SHARES: $29,942.78

PAYMENT ISSUED TO: Samuel Caldwell,
Sanford Co. Sheriff

He looked next at another:

CERTIFICATE OF STOCK
CASH-OUT RECEIPT

NAME OF STOCKHOLDER: Dr. Alfred W.
Preston

COMPANY: Procter & Gamble

NO. OF SHARES: 1,556

VALUE PER SHARE: $46.78

TOTAL VALUE OF SHARES: $72,789.68

PAYMENT ISSUED TO: Samuel Caldwell,
Sanford Co. Sheriff

There were six receipts in all, the other four for
stocks in Standard Oil, Southern Pacific Railroad, Aetna,

and the Pacific Lumber Company. All told, the stock values totaled $386,437.55, the shares of Standard Oil stock alone accounting for nearly half that sum.

The brazen bastard just cashed them out, Alfred thought, as disbelieving as he was indignant. *He just cashed them out under the pretext of a lawful seizure, took the receipts, and handed the cash over to Gibbs. No, no. He'll wait until after Gibbs has actually written a check against the account, as extra insurance against defection, and* then *hand over the money to Gibbs. Caldwell's too wily to be double-crossed.*

But why in the hell would he *keep* the receipts, rather than dispose of them at once?

In case something goes wrong. In case somebody does *actually manage to outbid Gibbs. He'll just have Gibbs convert the cash into cashiers' checks payable to the Sanford County Treasurer's Office, probably claiming he received a wildly excessive refund for property taxes paid on his store ("Looks like they put a decimal point in the wrong place!"), and then turn the checks and the stock receipts over to the Treasurer.*

It was the only explanation that made sense. But inasmuch as the market value of his estate was around $350,000, even by the appraisal of the County Assessor, it was virtually inconceivable that anyone should be inclined to outbid Gibbs.

I guess they were just covering all contingencies, he thought. Then something else occurred to him: *Why wasn't the money in the safe? Where in the hell else would Caldwell keep it? Under his pillow?*

The notion was laughable, but it was not lost on Alfred that, *had* the money been in the safe, his taking the contract and stock receipts would have almost certainly meant disaster: it was probable in the extreme that Caldwell would have gone to remove the cash from the safe prior to the auction, so that Gibbs could deposit the money into his bank account as soon as the event concluded.

Alfred looked now at the other document, a typewritten contract of just the sort he'd envisioned, a

Deep Cold

bilateral agreement between Caldwell and Gibbs. It read as follows:

AGREEMENT TO APPORTION PROCEEDS FROM SALE

WITNESS THIS AGREEMENT this __th day of March, 1886, by and between Herman Percy Gibbs ("Mr. Gibbs") and Samuel Edwin Caldwell ("Mr. Caldwell"), entered into knowingly and voluntarily by both parties hereto, that Mr. Gibbs shall pay to Mr. Caldwell forty percent (40%) of all proceeds derived from the sale of the estate formerly deeded to one Alfred W. Preston and now owned solely and exclusively by Mr. Gibbs, located at 212 Sycamore Lane, Timford, Connecticut, in the northeast corner of Sanford County, approximately at latitude 42 ° 30", longitude 84 ° 20", a half-mile southwest of the Phineas C. Loundsbury railroad bridge.

Mr. Gibbs shall apportion to Mr. Caldwell the above-referenced percentage of said proceeds in consideration of a debt owed to, and services rendered by or on behalf of, Samuel Caldwell, such services having been rendered for Mr. Gibbs's benefit and without prior compensation, and in exchange for a promise of future repayment.

The terms stated hereinabove constitute the entirety of this agreement between the parties hereto, and shall be enforced and interpreted in accordance with the laws of the State of Connecticut.

The contract had been signed by both Caldwell and Gibbs, but of course had yet to be notarized. That would have to wait until the deed had been transferred

309

into Gibbs's name - until, in other words, the estate had been stolen from Alfred.

But the signatures were enough, of course, particularly when combined with the stock receipts, the ledger from Jensen's, the bills of sale, the empty bag of flour, and the document prepared by Alfred's accountant. Taken cumulatively, they were as close to a smoking gun as one could reasonably hope to obtain.

Wishing for a pot of strong coffee, Alfred gathered up all the papers and tucked them away in his briefcase. Afraid to lie down lest he fall asleep, but also afraid to leave his room, he went to the bookcase on the other side of the room and selected a tome at random: *A Study in Scarlet*, by Arthur Conan Doyle.

He'd never heard of the author, but he supposed the book would keep his mind occupied until it was time to get ready.

XVII. THE AUCTION

The day was frigid, the snow having grown heavier overnight and heavier yet throughout the morning. The inclement weather notwithstanding, there was gathered on the courthouse steps and the street below a crowd of considerable size, consisting almost exclusively of men dressed in heavy overcoats and silk scarves and top hats. A few sported deerstalkers or wool caps. Under their coats most of the men wore suits and neckties or bow ties or ascots. One was even clad in a tuxedo, his coattails reaching clear to the backs of his Brooks Brothers shoes. The only two women present wore gowns of rich dupioni with delicate pearl-seed embroidery on the bodices, velvet capes around their shoulders, extravagant necklaces and opulent rings. The persons convened represented the most affluent and elite denizens of Sanford County and larger New England. Evidently word of the auction had spread far and wide.

Under the entablature, huddled around a tall podium made of birch wood, stood Andrew Denton, the

County Commissioner; Eli Stevenson, the County Assessor; George Arthur, the County Treasurer; and, at the front of the pack, Samuel Caldwell, the County Sheriff. A free-standing blackboard sat to the left of the podium. A large red banner had been hung from the arch over the courthouse doors, announcing the auction as if it were an annual raffle. And, indeed, the general mood seemed to be one of great excitement and levity, as perhaps under the circumstances only a herd of vultures could generate. The gluttony in their airs was as palpable as the snow swirling in the wind.

Only two men in the crowd stood out as unusual. One was a short, angular gentleman in his late fifties or early sixties, dressed humbly in a plaid flannel shirt, bright orange suspenders, wool pants fastened with hooks, and sullied work boots. Over his shirt he wore a threadbare cotton coat. He wore spectacles that hung on the edge of his nose, and was bald save for three curly white hairs. The other fellow was a man of far more elderly appearance, with a deformed nose and glossy, furrowed forehead and deep grooves under his eyes and in his cheeks. His hair was wavy, the color of cocoa beans. His eyelids bore a shade of fierce, unhealthy-looking scarlet, his lips a sickly, waxy sheen. He looked like a man who ought to be lying on his deathbed. This latter chap wore a black coat over a burgundy wool sweater and beige trousers, and brown leather boots on his feet. In his left hand he held a tan-colored briefcase. In his right he held a gnarled wooden cane with a brass knob.

The Commissioner stepped up to the podium, raised his hands in the air to silence the chattering crowd. "It's time to start!" he called over the din. "Let's get this thing going, everyone! We'll want to make it quick in view of the weather!" The crowd at last began to quiet down, their loud prattle now reduced to hushed murmurs. "Sheriff Caldwell has asked to administer the auction, and he'll open it with a reading of the sealed bids, so at this juncture I'll turn the stage over to him."

Denton now stepped aside so that Caldwell could take to the podium. "All right, everyone, all right. Now, first an important piece of information. My department and various other county agencies have received numerous inquiries regarding the very conduction of this proceeding. It's been asked how it can be held with Dr. Preston's still being at large. While I'm not at liberty to divulge any details, suffice it to say that this auction is taking place today in full accord with, and in total fidelity to, the laws of this County and the State of Connecticut. Let there be no aspersions cast, then, upon the legitimacy of the outcome of this afternoon's event, nor any doubts harbored about the legal validity of the resulting transaction.

"Now, with that out of the way, let's move onto business. The Clerk's office received a total of nine sealed bids. Incidentally, Mr. Feinstein is suffering from a bad head cold today and apologizes for his absence. In any case, as Mr. Denton indicated, we intend to make this proceeding as speedy as possible so we can all get out of this nasty weather and back indoors lickety-split. With that said, I shall commence to open the bids and the Commissioner shall record each bid and the bidder's name on the blackboard to my right. Remember, as stated in the rules governing this affair, those submitting sealed bids need not be present in order for their bids to qualify for consideration. In the event that a sealed bid proves to be the highest offer garnered, the bidder shall be notified by official letter and permitted fourteen calendar days to tender the amount of his or her bid to the office of the County Treasurer.

"Now, then, let's get on with it." Caldwell reached into a basket behind the podium and pulled out a small gray envelope, tore it open, and removed a thin strip of paper. "Albert Baker," he said. "Eighty-six thousand, eight hundred and forty-two dollars." The Commissioner promptly inscribed Mr. Baker's name and his rather paltry bid on the blackboard with a fat stick of white chalk. The Sheriff now reached into the basket again and fished out another envelope. "Ernest Fairchild. One hundred and sixty-four thousand, six hundred and seventy-seven dollars."

The recitations and recordings continued, until the last sealed bid, put in by Burt Holdbrook, was read:

"One hundred and forty-one thousand, five hundred dollars."

The Sheriff looked out at the crowd, thick flakes of snow collecting on the brim of his felt Keystone helmet. "All right, then," he said, glancing cursorily at the blackboard. "The highest sealed bid is Mr. Steernwheeler's of two hundred and thirty-seven thousand dollars. We'll now open the auction to higher bids, should there be any. And please keep in mind, folks, that, as per the rules set forth by the County Commission, all bids must be in increments of at least five thousand dollars."

"Two hundred and forty thousand!" cried a man near the front of the crowd. Everyone craned his neck to look at him, whispering amongst themselves. Who was it that could afford to pay such a sizable sum?

"Okay, I hear two hundred and forty thousand," said the Sheriff. "Can anyone go higher than that?"

Now a tall, slender gentleman with an ivory-capped scrimshaw cane stepped forward out of the

Michael Prescott

crowd. "I can go higher," he said with a sly, lop-sided smile. He raised his cane over his head and, with a ceremonious flourish of the rod and great pride in his tone, boldly proclaimed a bid of two hundred and forty-five thousand dollars.

"I hear two hundred and forty-five thousand dollars," Caldwell duly noted, and one might have read into his tone just the slightest trace of irritation. "I suspect nobody can go higher than that. So, two hundred and fifty thousand going once, *going twice –*"

"Two hundred and fifty thousand!" yelled the man in the plaid flannel shirt and soiled work boots from the back of the throng. Almost in unison, everyone in the legion of attendees turned to look at this small, bedraggled man who had previously gone almost entirely unnoticed. A few of the locals recognized him as Herman Gibbs, owner and sole proprietor of Timford's general store. And though all eyes were upon him, most of them quite disdainful, the lanky fellow in suspenders neither blushed nor looked away. On the contrary, he stood proudly with his shoulders arched back, beaming complacently from ear to ear. "I cashed in my railroad stocks and made a killing!"

A quiet but rancorous murmur ran through the crowd.

Sheriff Caldwell raised a hand to his forehead, as if trying to discern the location of this latest bidder. "Did I hear someone say two hundred and fifty thousand?" he asked.

"Yessir, Sheriff!" Gibbs called back. "You surely did!"

"Well," said the Sheriff, as if stunned by such a staggering offer, "I can't imagine we'll hear anything higher than *that*. So, going once, *going twice –*"

"Two hundred and fifty-five thousand!" the man with the scrimshaw cane barked obstinately. He appeared flummoxed, and more than a trifle annoyed.

"Two hundred and sixty!" yelled Gibbs.

Now the man with the scrimshaw cane looked positively affronted, even aggrieved. He waved his stick in the general direction of Gibbs. "Who the hell *are* you, anyhow? Where do you get off –"

"Do I hear higher than two hundred and sixty thousand?" Caldwell interrupted.

The man with the cane gritted his teeth. "Two hundred and sixty-three thousand!"

"Increments of five thousand or more," the Sheriff reminded him.

The slender man rapped his cane against one of the steps. "Blast! Two hundred and sixty-five thousand, then!"

Gibbs hesitated for a moment, and then announced a bid of two hundred and seventy thousand dollars.

"Bollocks!" cried the man with scrimshaw cane. He turned baleful eyes on Gibbs, who simply went on smiling with his hands stuffed in the pockets of his dirty wool pants. "Just who in the devil do you think you *are*, Mister? You look like a ragamuffin, a regular guttersnipe! You're an embarrassment –"

"Quiet down, sir," the Sheriff cautioned him with stern eyes. "We won't tolerate any berating or browbeating here today. We're auctioning an estate, not wagering on a cockfight." He took a breath and regrouped. "Very well, then, do I hear any bid higher than two hundred and seventy thousand dollars? If not, then going once, *going twice* –"

A small, hoarse voice with a German accent drifted through the crowd and up the courthouse steps: "I can go higher," it said. The man in the black overcoat and beige trousers, the man who looked on the brink of extinction, now cut a narrow path through the multitudes with his gnarled wooden cane.

"Excuse me, sir?" said the Sheriff, and there was now in his tone an unmistakable quality of profound vexation. "Did you say you can go *higher*?"

Michael Prescott

"That's right," said the old man with the German accent and brass-knobbed cane. He drew closer to the steps now, the awestruck crowd rather spontaneously parting to permit his passage. "I can go higher."

Sheriff Caldwell glared at him with cold, inimical eyes. "How much higher?"

"Three hundred and eighty-six thousand, four hundred and thirty-seven dollars and fifty-five cents."

Gasps went up in the crowd. One of the two women looked as if she might faint. The slender man with the scrimshaw cane loudly proffered that the whole auction was an artifice, a blatant machination.

"That bid is absurd, sir," the Sheriff said flatly, his gaze equal parts choler and bemusement. "Why, our fine Assessor here, Mr. Stevenson, has appraised the estate's value at approximately three hundred and fifty thousand dollars. Why on earth would you bid more than the market value of the estate, sir?"

"Because I own it," said the man in the black overcoat, his German accent having vanished, replaced now by a distinctly Yankee inflection. "And because that's precisely how much you and Mr. Gibbs stole from me to make certain that I won't own it much longer. Mr. Gibbs didn't cash in *his* railroad stocks. But you, Sheriff, cashed in *my* railroad stocks, as well as several others. Didn't you, you son of a bitch?"

The crowd, now utterly silent, watched with dazed, rapt eyes as the old decrepit man transformed himself piecemeal into a far more vigorous-looking fellow of much younger years: first by peeling putty from his nose; then by wiping makeup off his cheeks; then by using a handkerchief to erase the bright shine from his forehead; then by rubbing a layer of wax from his lips; and then, finally, by doffing his wig.

Alfred looked across the courthouse lawn and saw three State Police officers striding toward the steps. Two were quite short and plump, the other tall and lean. The short ones flanked the tall one, whom Alfred surmised was Richard Alderson, the Chief Inspector of the CSP.

"Preston!" Caldwell cried, looking about frantically for assistance, perhaps from deputies who weren't there. "That's Alfred Preston, the professor who murdered his wife! He's a fugitive! Detain him at once!"

"I've evidence in this case," said Alfred loudly but calmly, lifting the briefcase into the air, "proving beyond a shadow of a doubt that Sheriff Caldwell and Herman Gibbs first conspired to murder my beloved wife and then colluded to guarantee that Mr. Gibbs's bid on my estate would be the highest offered at today's auction, that the two men might later sell the property and split the proceeds. I have, furthermore, irrefutable proof that Sheriff Caldwell embezzled a portion of my assets during their seizure in order to finance the venture on Mr. Gibbs's behalf."

A general frenzy now prevailed, the crowd shouting and jeering while Caldwell and the other county officials simply stood flabbergasted upon the courthouse steps. The three officers of the State Police were jostling their way through the assembly, nearly to the path now. Caldwell saw them, looked back at Alfred, and drew his side arm. "Drop that case and put your hands in the air!" he commanded, pointing the gun at Alfred. "Drop it or I'll shoot you dead where you stand!"

"You'll do no such thing," said the Chief Inspector as he climbed the courthouse steps, his constables in tow. He opened a billfold and flashed his identification badge. "Richard Alderson, Chief Inspector of the Connecticut State Police. Holster that weapon immediately, Sheriff."

Caldwell was beginning to sweat now, assuming the mien of a trapped animal. Reluctantly, he holstered his weapon. "Don't you understand, Officer? That man's a fugitive! A murder suspect! You yourself informed me by letter just a few days ago that your department had taken him into custody! Just what in the hell is going on here?"

Then, suddenly, Gibbs made a run for it. Alderson spotted him and ordered one of his constables to give chase. He turned back to Caldwell and said, "I sent you no such letter, Sheriff. But I *did* receive a letter from one Walter Givens to the effect that you and Mr. Gibbs are responsible for the death of Julia Preston."

Caldwell was now hopelessly and perfectly nonplussed, as confounded and agitated as any man Alfred had ever seen. He couldn't help but smile.

"You, sir!" called the Inspector to Alfred. "Are you Walter Givens?"

"I am," Alfred replied, coming closer. "But I'm also Alfred W. Preston."

"How do you mean, sir?"

"I mean that I wrote the letter to which you referred, using an alias to protect myself. But I have in this case all the evidence I described in my letter, all the evidence needed to exonerate me and implicate Caldwell and Gibbs both."

The constable who'd chased Gibbs had caught him and now marched him up the steps, under the entablature. "Here he is, Chief," said the constable. Both men were winded. "I found this in his pocket." The constable held up a blank check.

"Just hold him there," Alderson said. "And put that check in an evidence bag." Then, to Alfred: "Bring your case up here and show me what you've got. It had better be *very* good, sir, or I'll have my handcuffs on you before you can so much as sneeze."

Alfred walked up the steps and took his briefcase to Alderson. Caldwell and Gibbs looked on in horror and disbelief. The Commissioner, Assessor, and Treasurer had stepped aside, watching the burlesque affair unfold with a kind of detached bewilderment. The crowd had largely dispersed at the instruction of the other constable, but a few busybodies stubbornly remained.

The Inspector carried the case over to the podium, unfastened the snaps, and opened it. He

Michael Prescott

removed the stock receipts one by one, studying each with a careful if skeptical eye, and then the contract. And then the druggist's ledger. And then the bills of sale, pink carbonated copies impressed with a metal stylus. And then the burlap sack, turning it over and reading the words stamped on its underside. And then, finally, the document prepared by Alfred's accountant.

He considered for a moment, scratching his chin, then returned the papers and the sack to the briefcase and turned to the three men standing off to the side. "Which of you is the Treasurer?" he asked.

"I am, Officer," said George Arthur, stepping forward.

"What was the total value of the assets Sheriff Caldwell seized from Dr. Preston's various accounts and turned over to your office? Do you recall?"

Arthur blushed, flustered and trying to think. "Um," he said, lifting a hand to his cheek. "Yes, I do, as a matter of fact. I believe it was something on the order of $2.7 million, sir. Officer."

327

"That's excluding the value of the estate, yes?"

"Yes. That's only counting Dr. Preston's liquid assets and various other holdings, such as his stocks and bonds."

Alderson nodded thoughtfully and turned now to Gibbs. "Is there any particular reason you required that four hundred milligrams of arsenic be delivered to your store, Mr. Gibbs?"

Gibbs swallowed thickly and licked his bone-dry lips. "I had a rat problem," he said. His voice was a strained, pathetic whisper. "A really, tremendously awful rat problem."

"I figure you could kill half the rats on the eastern seaboard with that much arsenic," the Inspector quipped dryly. "And why, pray tell, did you flee the scene after Dr. Preston here announced that he had evidence implicating you in his wife's murder?"

Beads of sweat had risen on Gibbs's brow, despite the freezing cold. He shifted awkwardly on his feet. "I was afraid," he said. "I was afraid the Sheriff had done something underhanded and would try to pin it on me. I worried I wouldn't be believed."

The Inspector looked at Gibbs as one might regard a child denying the theft of a cookie with his hand still in the jar. "Uh huh. I see." He turned now to Caldwell. "And you, Sheriff," he said. "Any reason in particular you kept the stock certificate receipts rather than relinquishing them to the Treasurer along with the cash?"

"I just hadn't gotten around to it yet," Caldwell said. Unlike Gibbs, who now appeared utterly defeated, the Sheriff remained righteously indignant. "Why are you even listening to this rubbish?" he demanded. "The man's a murderer! He's been wanted across the whole state for over a month now! He –"

"Be quiet, Sheriff." Alderson probed him with icy, penetrating eyes. "Mind explaining *this*?" Alderson held up the contract between Caldwell and Gibbs.

Caldwell didn't hesitate. "I knew Herman had cashed in his railroad stocks and so was likely to put in the highest bid on the estate. We only drafted that contract yesterday, between ourselves. We just wanted to be prepared once the sale was final."

Alderson looked at Gibbs. "Is that your story, as well?"

Gibbs simply nodded.

"And neither of you thought it wise to consult an attorney with such a huge sum at stake?"

"Trying to save money," Caldwell muttered.

Alderson scowled at him. "What was that, Sheriff?"

"I said we were trying to save money."

"I see."

There was a brief silence, and then Alderson turned to his constables, unhooked his handcuffs and handed them to the one on his right. "Detain Sheriff

Caldwell, Mr. Gibbs, and Dr. Preston. Take them to the local jailhouse and put them each in a separate cell. I'll be along shortly."

The constables dutifully complied, handcuffing each of the three men. Alfred did not protest. Gibbs was near tears and mumbling about how he'd done nothing wrong. Caldwell, without quite resisting, continued to rant that Alfred was a fugitive and a murderer and that all his so-called "evidence" amounted to diddly-squat, was pure bunkum.

The two constables led the three men to a horse-drawn carriage and instructed each to get inside.

Fifteen minutes later, Alfred was sitting in the very jail cell to which Caldwell and his deputies had meant to escort him some thirty-three days earlier.

XVIII. THE OLD NOOSE

The cell was drab and bare, with nothing to sit on but a concrete bench. The constable had removed his handcuffs, at least, leaving him free to rest his chin on his hands. He sat and waited, contemplating all that had happened in the foregoing weeks. The waiting was almost as agonizing as the wait for the auction had been, seconds dragging on like minutes and minutes like hours.

He was not a particularly religious or devout man, Alfred Wilson Preston, but he did believe in a benevolent God and a hereafter. He held a deep faith, moreover, that his late wife was up in Heaven, suffering along with him but at the same time enjoying bounteous riches and eternal bliss. He got down on his knees now, on the hard, dirty cement floor of his cell, and folded his hands together in prayer. "Please, God," he whispered, "let things turn out all right. Let the men in whose hands my fate rests learn the truth and reach a just decision. Not for my sake, Lord, but for Julia's. I beg of you. Amen."

He rose to his feet and began to pace around the cramped cell, chewing his fingernails down to the quick. At some point he heard voices in the corridor outside his cell. One was Alderson's, and another was that, Alfred thought, of the constable who had driven the carriage to the jailhouse. They were speaking quietly, and Alfred couldn't quite make out their words. Then there were footsteps down the corridor, away from Alfred's cell, followed by another set coming in the other direction. He began to sit up, expecting either the Inspector or the constable to release him, and then the footsteps stopped just short of his cell. He heard Alderson say, "Caldwell."

A brief moment of silence ensued, then a stirring in the cell adjacent to Alfred's. "Yes? I trust you've come to apologize and let me go?" Caldwell's voice, low and defiant.

"On the contrary, Sheriff. We've already spoken to Gibbs, and the District Attorney. Gibbs has agreed to testify against you in exchange for a more lenient sentence."

"Testify *against* me?" Alfred relished the ire in Caldwell's voice. "On what grounds, dammit? I've done nothing wrong!"

"He initially denied any wrongdoing on his own part, as well. Then we told him that we investigated the bank account he opened yesterday afternoon in Georgetown. The blank check he had on him made *that* task quite simple. The account had seven dollars in it, Sheriff Caldwell. Seven measly dollars. And yet he was prepared to write a check against it in the amount of nearly three hundred thousand dollars in order to purchase Dr. Preston's estate. Quite remarkable, wouldn't you say?"

"I know nothing about any check. Nothing about any bank account in Georgetown, either."

"Of course you don't, Sheriff. Anymore than you knew about Gibbs's regular orders of arsenide compounds from a druggist in Bridgeport, compounds containing increasingly greater measures of arsenic."

"How in God's name would I know about *those*, Inspector?"

"The same way you knew Gibbs's would be the highest bid at the auction. Because the two of you colluded, just as Dr. Preston maintains."

Q.E.D., Alfred thought.

"You've no proof of that."

"I think the contract suffices as such proof, Sheriff. And besides, there's no question you embezzled a large portion of Dr. Preston's assets during your seizure of them. We found over three hundred and eighty-five thousand dollars in cash in the saddlebag on your horse. Any reason you might stash it there if you truly intended to relinquish it to the County Treasurer's office?"

Caldwell was silent for a moment, and then, incredibly: "It seemed as safe a place as any."

"As safe as under your pillow?"

"Pardon me?"

"We investigated your home, Sheriff. It seems that in your haste you left behind a thousand-dollar bill. It was poking out from your pillowcase."

More silence from Caldwell, but Alfred could almost hear him seething. *My God*, he thought. *The fool actually stashed the treasure under his pillow, after all!*

"We also noticed that fine sketch of a lavish ranch house on your drafting table. I understand you used to be an architect. Did you perchance have any plans to use the loot to abscond to the West and finance the construction of such a charming abode? One of your filing clerks told us you submitted a request just yesterday for two weeks of personal leave. Two weeks during which your absence in town would be far less conspicuous than it might have been otherwise. Quite an interesting coincidence, wouldn't you say, Sheriff Caldwell?"

"I don't know what you're talking about," the Sheriff muttered. There was no defiance left in his tone now, but only bitter resignation.

"You'd no intention of honoring your cloak-and-dagger deal with Gibbs, had you? And why would you? Even if the two of you had split the proceeds fifty-fifty, right down the middle, you still would've come out in far worse shape than if you'd simply fled with the cash in your saddlebag. And at a mere forty percent of the proceeds? Why, it hardly would have been worth your trouble, would it?

"And I must appreciate the irony that while you purported to draft the contract to protect your own financial interests, in fact you did so merely to lend further credibility to the notion that you *did* intend to make good on the deal. To add that... how shall I put it? Extra touch of plausibility to your deceit of deceits. Or, more colloquially, to keep Gibbs off your scent. Which is only further proof of your intent to embezzle the money and keep it for yourself.

"As for the stock receipts and the contract, I can only assume you held onto them in case Gibbs demanded to see them this morning, as proof that you'd done the deed and – pardon the rhyme – had no tricks up your sleeve. But it seems the documents went missing in the night, doesn't it, Sheriff? And, unfortunately for you, you didn't bother to check on them before leaving home this morning."

"I want a lawyer," Caldwell said feebly. He sounded as if he were asking for a glass of water.

"The judge will appoint one for you, unless you wish to hire your own. With money which actually belongs to *you*, that is." Alderson paused here, and Alfred could hear him squatting so that he'd be eye-level with Caldwell. "We've got you nailed on embezzlement flat-out, just on the physical evidence alone. And with the help of Gibbs's testimony, the District Attorney should have little trouble making out a case for either conspiracy to commit murder or accessory to murder, whichever would carry the stiffer sentence. That means you'll most likely spend the rest of your natural life behind bars, Sheriff. But if you want to cooperate and spare the State the trouble of trying you, I'm sure the DA might be amenable to a plea deal. What do you think, Caldwell? Are you ready to give up the act?"

"I want a lawyer," Caldwell repeated, his voice even fainter now.

The Inspector stood up. "Very well. You'll be arraigned in the morning, at which time the judge will appoint an attorney to represent you until you can hire one of your choosing, if you're so inclined."

Caldwell said nothing, and now Alderson came to Alfred's cell. "Dr. Preston?"

Alfred rose wearily but eagerly from the bench and walked to the bars of his cell. "Yes, Inspector?"

"I assume you overheard my little chat with Sheriff Caldwell?"

"I did, sir, yes." There were tears in Alfred's eyes.

"On behalf of the Connecticut State Police and the Governor himself, Dr. Preston, I wish to extend you my most heartfelt apologies for the incomprehensible hardship you must have endured over the past month, as well as my deepest condolences on the loss of your wife. We can't even imagine the adversities you've suffered as a result of your unjust arrest, much less the grief you've borne over the tragic manner in which your wife was taken from you."

He extended a hand through two of the bars, and Alfred shook it. Tears ran down his pale cheeks. "You've nothing to apologize for," he said. "You did nothing wrong. Only Sheriff Caldwell did. And Herman Gibbs."

The Inspector smiled dolefully. "Nevertheless, sir, we are all deeply sorry for what's happened." He turned now and called to a constable, "Edmund, come and open this cell, please."

Edmund came and unlocked the cell door, then rejoined his colleague near the front exit, where the two men conversed in low voices and one of them lit a pipe.

Alfred hesitated, as if still incredulous that it was all really over.

"You're free to go, Dr. Preston," said the Inspector. He gestured down the hallway. "The door at the end of the corridor is open, and you'll find the gates to your home unlocked. Constable Bradshaw will drive you there in the carriage."

Still crying, Alfred stepped out of the cell. He started for the door, then wiped his eyes and turned around. He looked at Alderson, half-curious and half-afraid. He opened his mouth to speak and then closed it again.

"Something the matter, Dr. Preston?"

"Inspector," Alfred said reluctantly, "you never asked me how I came by the stock receipts or the contract. Or how I obtained the ledger and bills of sale from Jensen."

Alderson smiled again, this time more cheerily, and gave Alfred a subtle wink. "It hardly matters, sir. As far as the CSP is concerned, you're innocent of any wrongdoing."

Alfred nodded, began to turn away, and then hesitated again. "May I ask you two things, Inspector?"

"Certainly," said Alderson.

"Why do you suppose Caldwell and Gibbs chose to poison my wife slowly, over time, rather than all at once?"

The Inspector smirked. "Would a man as intelligent as you commit murder in so obvious a manner? Or would he, instead, try to conceal the victim's death as the result of a prolonged illness, blithely unaware that a thorough autopsy can reveal even trace amounts of arsenic in the decedent's tissue or blood?"

Alfred nodded. He'd suspected as much himself but merely wanted to hear Alderson's opinion of the matter.

"And your other question?" the Inspector asked.

Alfred cleared his throat. "Why did Gibbs snitch on Sheriff Caldwell? He could have denied the whole thing, just as Caldwell did, and taken his chances at trial."

"The evidence against him was overwhelming, and he knew it. Once I threatened to have the dusting of flour at the bottom of the bag you supplied tested for arsenic, he simply cracked under the pressure."

"But still," Alfred pressed, "he had nothing to lose by denying any involvement in the crime. So why do you suppose he caved?"

"Of course he had something to lose," the Inspector said. "He had a choice between life in prison and... what do you boys call it down here in the country?" He chuckled grimly. "Ah, yes: the old noose."

Alfred smiled wanly and favored Alderson with a slight nod. The Inspector returned the gesture, then made his way to the rear exit of the jailhouse, whistling softly.

Alfred turned and plodded down the hallway on heavy, aching feet. Constable Bradshaw opened the door for him, and he stepped out into the frosty night air, a truly free man at last.

XIX. EPILOGUE (SAYING GOOD-BYE)

The cemetery was situated at the top of a steep hill, which Alfred now climbed in his own lace-up ankle boots and beaver-fur coat. He carried a bouquet of flowers in his right hand. A heavy snow fell from clouds as black as raven's feathers. The sun was just setting.

He crested the hill, searched about for a minute, and located Julia's grave. It was marked by a simple, unadorned slate tombstone. It bore only her name and the dates of her birth and death. Alfred regretted this deeply, wishing he could have ordered that it also be inscribed with the words "Loving Wife and Loyal Friend."

"Hello, love," he said, his words carried away on a high wind. "I never got a chance to bid you a proper farewell, so I'm afraid this is the best I can do. I know it's late coming, and I wish so desperately that I could have come sooner. But it simply... it simply wasn't possible. I'm sure you can understand, dear."

The wind howled, bending the branches of nearby trees and rattling the few leaves they had sprouted. Snow whirled about his feet, blew up against the headstone.

"I did it, Julia," he whispered. "I caught the men who killed you. The evil fiends who took you from me. And they'll never see the light of day again."

All at once he collapsed to his knees and began to sob into his hands. The sky was almost dark now, a crescent moon faintly visible through the clouds. "I'm sorry!" he wailed, his chest hitching as tears streamed down his cheeks. "I'm so sorry, Julia!"

Another violent gust of wind blasted his face and swept his hair back. Slowly, very slowly, he composed himself and ran the sleeve of his coat across his eyes.

He leaned down and carefully placed the bouquet of flowers at the foot of the headstone.

"Rest in peace, my dear," he said to his wife. "Rest in peace."

NOTES ON "FORTUITOUS"

Let me preface this afterword of sorts by saying that, unless you either loved "The Fortuitous Death of Dr. Alfred W. Preston" or simply harbor a deep curiosity about the more arcane aspects of life in rural New England *circa* 1886 (particularly with regard to crime, medicine, or law), these notes will likely bore you to tears. Thus, if you do not fall into one of the categories described above, please feel entirely free at this point to simply close the book and either shelve it or lend it to a friend or relative. For the rest of you, off we go.

"Fortuitous" has a long and, to me at least, rather interesting history. I began work on the story almost ten years ago, intrigued by the notion of a tale incorporating elements of both the film *The Fugitive* and Edgar Allan Poe's "The Premature Burial." I envisioned a fairly simple, relatively short crime story, a murder-mystery of sorts, set in late nineteenth-century New

England. I imagined it would run about thirty, maybe thirty-five pages in length.

I got about four pages into it before setting it aside, partly because of various distractions (including other projects) but mostly because I'd begun to realize that, to be told properly, the tale would need to be much larger in scope and require extensive research into a variety of rather obscure subjects, ranging from the symptoms and pathology of arsenic poisoning to the prevailing medical practices of the time period to the mechanics of elaborate embezzlement and money laundering. It would also, I surmised, require at least a rudimentary knowledge of more mundane but equally important historical phenomena, such as the fashion and architectural trends of the era, the state of various technologies, the commercial availability and costs of sundry products and services, the dominant vernacular of the region, and, perhaps worst of all, the inner workings of law enforcement agencies, governmental institutions, and municipal bureaucracies.

Michael Prescott

I have always loathed anything more than cursory research where creative endeavors are concerned, finding it as daunting as I do dull. (Maybe that's why most of my stories are set in the present day, populated by lower- to middle-class American characters, and feature as their thematic centerpieces addiction, mental illness, or both.) It was largely inevitable, then, that, after writing another five pages or so of the story a year or two later, I abandoned it for the second time. When the original draft of the first nine pages of the story was subsequently irretrievably lost, its fate as a permanently unfinished and discarded work seemed pretty much sealed.

And then, in the fall of 2012, I found myself at an impasse in a new short story I was writing, a story intended to be part of a forthcoming compilation I planned to call *Deep Cold* (mostly because all of the tales would be set in the wintertime, featuring snow and cold weather as prominent motifs). It also occurred to me that, with only eight stories averaging about ten pages in length, I didn't have nearly enough material to constitute a collection of respectable or conventional size. Quite suddenly, for the first time in more than six years, I remembered that pesky, complicated crime story on which I'd given up nearly a decade before. With great reluctance, and largely out of necessity (I had no other ideas for a story at the time, much less for enough stories to fill up all that empty space), I once more took up "The Fortuitous Death of Alfred W. Preston," starting as I had to from scratch.

I composed what would later become the first two chapters quite quickly, doing the necessary research piecemeal as I wrote. Then, as I ventured deeper into the ever-thickening plot, and the cast of characters grew progressively larger, and – worst of all, of course – the required research expanded to unsettling proportions, the march of my pen across the page, as it were, began steadily to slow.

I knew, vaguely, where I wanted to go, how I wanted things to all basically work out, but found myself again and again at a total loss as to how to get there. I grew increasingly overwhelmed by the ever-expanding scope of the project, and increasingly confounded by the logistical obstacles in my path. The particulars of the conspiracy between Caldwell and Gibbs proved especially thorny and elusive. I spent countless sleepless hours in bed, tossing and turning, trying to little avail to work them out at least satisfactorily if not ideally - that is, in a way that the reader was likely to find both factually believable and fittingly crafty, making for a sensational climax. And, of course, in a fashion that would gratify me as the author.

A big part of my problem was that I didn't know beans about stocks, bonds, or finances in general, much less their nature and operation in the late nineteenth century. (I've never purchased a share of stock in my life, and wouldn't have the first clue about how to buy, trade, or sell one.) Having grown utterly weary of research by this point, but determined that the elements of the conspiracy should be as authentic as the speech and dress of the characters, I enlisted the aid of one of my closest friends, Matthew Brummond, a fellow attorney who, though hardly an expert on such matters, knew far more about them than I did. His assistance proved invaluable, and without it, "Fortuitous" may once again have been doomed to oblivion.

I am still not particularly thrilled with the mechanism by which Caldwell purported to conspire with Gibbs to slowly snuff out Alfred's wife and divest Alfred of his estate (I would have preferred something cleverer), but trust me when I tell you that it is far more artful and persuasive than it was in previous iterations. Nevertheless, I *am* very pleased with the story's denouement, the drama of it and preceding suspense, and, most of all, the palpable and righteous relish Alfred enjoys when he exposes Caldwell and Gibbs for the murderous fraudsters that they are.

The astute reader will have noticed that, despite all my thorough and taxing research, I still took some artistic liberties with certain historical and geographical details (nearly all the towns referenced in the story are fictional, as well as Sanford County itself), in particular the existence and size of the Connecticut State Police in 1886. In point of fact, while one of the oldest state police forces in the Union, it did not originate until 1903, when five men were hired to enforce state liquor and vice laws, for which task they were paid three dollars a day. It is also quite unlikely that a constable's badge would not have borne his name as well as his precinct and division numbers, and at least fairly improbable than an officer of a state police department, even in nineteenth-century New England, would have been called a "constable." Furthermore, it is less than certain that police officers even in then relatively well-populated cities such as Middletown, much less sheriffs and deputies in more rustic parts of New England, would have at that time carried side arms in the regular course of their duties. (A possible solecism of far lesser magnitude and import is the Middletown secretary's use of a rubber ink stamp to notarize Alfred's letters; I was unable to determine whether such a tool was yet in common use back then, or even existed.)

An anachronism much less glaring (except perhaps to Holmes fanatics) but decidedly cheekier than any of the preceding is the reference in Chapter XVI to

Sir Arthur Conan Doyle's *A Study in Scarlet*, which was not published until 1887 and did not enjoy wide circulation in the United States until the early twentieth century. These inconvenient facts aside, I simply couldn't resist the nod to that particular work of Doyle's, which, as well as Poe's "Premature Burial" and "Murders in the Rue Morgue" (and, to a lesser extent, Stephen King's "Autopsy Room Four"), served as a great inspiration for the story. More trivially, it is unclear to me when the expression "Rats!" entered popular usage as an interjection conveying frustration or dismay. (All my efforts to identify its date of origin were in vain.) But, as with *Scarlet*, I just couldn't resist Jensen's dropping such a cutesy if less than terribly clever pun.

Being an attorney (albeit one with virtually no experience in the field of wills, trusts, and estates), I felt a heightened duty to get my legal facts straight. However, being a writer, I also felt completely justified in simply inventing a statute which, while rather draconian, does not seem entirely implausible for the era. I here refer, of course, to the state law whereby the Sanford County officials were permitted to auction the estate of a man merely incarcerated for a capital crime, restoring it to his ownership only in the event of an acquittal (or, presumably, a subsequent dismissal of the charges). While I did not research the subject (forgive me), I suspect it much more likely that possession of all property belonging to the accused, barring any seized during a lawful search, would have remained with him until or unless he was convicted, whereupon he likely could have made private arrangements with family or friends to manage all his assets, home included, during his incarceration. Or, at the very least, ownership of such items simply would have been conveyed to his next of kin or any heir(s) identified in his will. All these probabilities notwithstanding, without the fictional statute in question there would have been no feasible premise for the kind of story I wished to write, and so, once again, I simply exercised literary license.

As for the contract between Caldwell and Gibbs, it was probably valid as written, and a court likely would have enforced it in the event that suit was brought by Caldwell. This is only the case, however, because of the inclusion of the provision that Caldwell had loaned money to and performed services for Gibbs *in exchange for a promise of future repayment*. Otherwise, there would have been legally insufficient consideration for the contract to be enforceable. Once again, I owe a debt of gratitude to my lawyer friend, Matt Brummond, for pointing out this picayune detail. (Especially where legal minutiae are concerned, but with respect to most other matters as well, his mind works like a steel trap while mine works more like a broken sieve.)

Ironically, as little as I know about medicine, I am confident that nearly all of the medical details in the story are factually and historically accurate. The symptoms Julia experiences as a result of first gradual and then more abrupt and acute arsenic poisoning are wholly realistic, and those which Alfred suffers after being bitten by the (fictional) pit viper are equally based on solid fact. Phenol was indeed a prevalent antiseptic, if not the one most commonly used for the disinfection of serious wounds, in late nineteenth-century America. Likewise, ether was a highly popular anesthetic, probably the *most* popular drug of its kind, among the medical community of that era. One rather gross exception to the overall accuracy of the medical details in the novella is the Brainbridge doctor's explanation of how Alfred managed to survive the snakebite. If there is any truth whatsoever to the notion that extreme cold prevents or even slows the spreading of venom throughout the bloodstream of one bitten by a poisonous snake, it is pure and utter coincidence.

I also feel quite assured that I got at least most of the economic and transactional details right. I conducted fairly painstaking research into the average costs of various products and services in the place and period in which the story is set, in particular those of hotel rooms, lodging in boarding houses, articles of clothing, and quality horses. I am less certain that the values of Alfred's various stock shares were realistic for the time, but ultimately judged them sufficiently plausible to make use of their mathematical expediency.

In addition, an estate then valued at $350,000 would be equivalent to an estate today worth, I imagine, at least ten million dollars, making Alfred one exceptionally wealthy fellow.

It is my hope that none of the anachronisms or any factual missteps distracted inordinately from the reader's enjoyment of the story, and that, for all my artistic liberties and (hopefully minor) blunders, he or she was able to suspend disbelief throughout it. I also hope very much that, at a bare minimum, I succeeded in capturing the feel and spirit of the time period, locale, and various ilks of people who lived in them.

For all I have said in these notes on the laborious creation and possible faults of "Fortuitous," I am enormously proud of the story, deeming it one of my finest creative efforts to date. It is my further hope, Dear Reader, that you concur.

Michael J. Prescott
February 16, 2013

Michael Prescott

Made in United States
Troutdale, OR
12/04/2023